Jesse had meant the kiss to show Sarah that he was too wild for a woman like her. Maybe even scare her a little, so she'd stop looking at him with those damn stars in her eyes.

So much for that idea.

The kiss had stunned him.

That was the only word for the torrent of emotions it had sent tumbling through him— tenderness and protectiveness and a raw, hot need. He wanted to pull her close, safeguard her from whatever had put that lost look in her eyes, keep her safe and warm and…loved.

Now *he* was the one who was scared. What was he thinking, kissing a soft, fragile, forever kind of woman like her? She deserved far better than a rough lawman with wild blood running through his veins.

Trouble was, he didn't want to stay away from *her*. Damn his hide, he wanted her more than ever.…

Dear Reader,

They say that March comes in like a lion, and we've got six
fabulous books to help you start this month off with a bang.
Ruth Langan's popular series, THE LASSITER LAW, continues
with *Banning's Woman*. This time it's the Banning sister, a freshman
congresswoman, whose life is in danger. And to the rescue…
handsome police officer Christopher Banning, who's vowed to
get Mary Bren out of a stalker's clutches—and *into* his arms.

ROMANCING THE CROWN continues with Marie Ferrarella's
The Disenchanted Duke, in which a handsome private investigator—
with a strangely royal bearing—engages in a spirited battle with
a beautiful bounty hunter to locate the missing crown prince.
And in Linda Winstead Jones's *Capturing Cleo,* a wary detective
investigating a murder decides to close in on the prime suspect—
the dead man's sultry and seductive ex-wife—by pursuing her
romantically. Only problem is, where does the investigation end
and romance begin? Beverly Bird continues our LONE STAR
COUNTRY CLUB series with *In the Line of Fire*, in which a
policewoman investigating the country club explosion must
team up with an ex-mobster who makes her pulse race in more
ways than one. You won't want to miss RaeAnne Thayne's second
book in her OUTLAW HARTES miniseries, *Taming Jesse James,*
in which reformed bad-boy-turned-sheriff Jesse James Harte
puts his life—not to mention his heart—on the line for lovely
schoolteacher Sarah MacKenzie. And finally, in *Keeping Caroline*
by Vickie Taylor, a tragedy pushes a man back toward the wife he'd
left behind—and the child he never knew he had.

Enjoy all of them! And don't forget to come back next month when
the excitement continues in Silhouette Intimate Moments.

Yours,

Leslie J. Wainger
Executive Senior Editor

Please address questions and book requests to:
Silhouette Reader Service
U.S.: 3010 Walden Ave., P.O. Box 1325, Buffalo, NY 14269
Canadian: P.O. Box 609, Fort Erie, Ont. L2A 5X3

Taming
Jesse James
RAEANNE
THAYNE

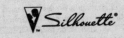

Published by Silhouette Books

America's Publisher of Contemporary Romance

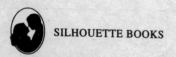 **SILHOUETTE BOOKS**

ISBN 0-373-27209-X

TAMING JESSE JAMES

Copyright © 2002 by RaeAnne Thayne

This edition published by arrangement with Harlequin Books S.A.

Visit Silhouette at www.eHarlequin.com

Printed in U.S.A.

RAEANNE THAYNE

lives in a graceful old Victorian nestled in the rugged mountains of northern Utah, along with her husband and two young children. Her books have won numerous honors, including several Readers' Choice awards and a RITA Award nomination by the Romance Writers of America. RaeAnne loves to hear from readers. She can be reached through her Web site at www.raeannethayne.com or at P.O. Box 6682, North Logan, UT 84341.

To Maureen Green, Chris Christensen,
Jennifer Black and Carrie Robinson,
my sisters and my best friends.
For all the clothes, parenting tips, yard sales
and side-aching, milk-out-of-your-nose laughfests
we've shared over the years. I love you!

Chapter 1

Jesse James Harte was in deep, deep trouble.

"You playin' or are you just gonna sit there lookin' pretty?" the scrappier of his two opponents asked with a fearless smirk.

Jesse glared at his cards, trying to figure out his options. They didn't look any cheerier than they had a few moments ago.

"Come on. We're waitin'."

"Yeah, yeah. Hold your water." He looked at his hand one last time, then back at the two troublemakers across the table from him. His throat was parched and he needed a drink in the worst way, but he didn't dare turn his back on these two desperadoes. Not for a second. The two of them were as terrifying as any hardened criminal he'd ever come up against.

Finally he knew he would have to do something, and quick. He set down the only possible card he could—jack of hearts. As soon as it left his hand, he knew it was a mistake. A triumphant shout rang through the room and a queen of hearts slapped onto his jack.

His niece Lucy gave a shriek of excitement. "Ha! That was her last card. You lose, Uncle Jess! Told ya you'd never be able to beat Dylan at crazy eights. She's the best. The absolute best."

"The winner and still undefeated champ-i-on!" Dylan Webster, Lucy's stepsister of less than a month, jumped from the chair across from his desk and did a little hip-jiggling victory dance around his office.

Jesse leaned back in his chair and watched their celebratory gyrations out of narrowed eyes. "You cheated. I can't figure out how, but you must have cheated. Worse than a couple of Wild West card sharks, that's what you are. Come in here after school acting all sweet and innocent, saying you just stopped in to say hello, and then you bilk me out of two Snickers bars. You think I don't know what's going on?"

Dylan batted her eyes at him. "Who, us? Would we do something like that?" That one was going to be a heartbreaker just like her mom, when she put on a few more years.

"I ought to lock you both up right now and throw away the key," Jesse growled. "Teach you to mess with the Salt River chief of police."

The girls just giggled at him.

"Come on. Best two out of three." He scooped up the cards and started shuffling them. "Better yet, I'll teach you how to play a real game. How about blackjack?"

"We already know how to play," Dylan assured him.

"How about acey-deucy? No? Sit back down, then." He did a fancy little flourish with the cards that sent them cascading between his hands in a rainbow. His little card trick was rewarded with two pairs of wide eyes.

"Cool!" Lucy exclaimed. "Where'd you learn to do that?"

"Years of practice, beating the pants off your dad. He stinks at cards. Always has. And you can tell him I said so, too." He grinned and she giggled back.

"Will you teach me how to do it?"

"Sure, if you give me the first bite of that Snickers bar."

Before she could answer, a knock sounded at the door.

"Yeah?"

His dispatcher, receptionist and all-around pain in the neck shoved open the door and stood in the doorway, all four feet ten inches of her.

"Chief, you got company," Lou Montgomery barked.

"Yeah?"

"Says it's important."

"Send him in, then."

"Her," a new voice interjected. Compared to Lou's rotgut-rough voice, this one was as soft and smooth as water rippling over rocks. He knew that voice. He opened his mouth to answer, but before he could, the girls beat him to it.

"Ms. McKenzie!" they shrieked in unison, and rushed to greet his visitor, their fourth-grade teacher. She gave them a strained smile but accepted their hugs graciously.

"What are you doing here?" Dylan asked.

The pretty teacher looked uncomfortable. "I...I just had some business to discuss with Chief Harte."

Something she obviously didn't want to share with two nosy little girls. Before the terrible twosome could interrogate her about it, Jesse stepped in. "Ladies, I'll have to take a raincheck on the poker lessons. Aren't you supposed to be cleaning out the stalls at the clinic, anyway?"

They both groaned, but picked up their backpacks. "Bye, Ms. McKenzie," they chimed in unison.

"Thanks for the Snickers bars." Dylan smirked at Jesse on her way out the door.

As soon as they left, Ms. McKenzie raised a delicate eyebrow at him. "Poker lessons?"

Despite that sexy voice of hers, the schoolmarm tone still made him feel as if he'd just been caught throwing spitballs. He cleared his throat. "Uh, guilty. What can I say? I'm a bad influence. Sit down. How can I help you?"

After a brief hesitation, she walked across the office with that slight, barely perceptible limp that had been driving him crazy with curiosity since she'd moved to town at the beginning of the school year.

She slipped into the chair across the desk from him and folded her hands carefully on her lap, her green eyes focused on some point just to the left of his face.

He fought the urge to look over his shoulder to see what she found so fascinating back there. Judging by their few brief encounters since her arrival in Salt River eight months ago, he had the uncomfortable feeling she wasn't looking at anything in particular, just away from him.

For some reason, he seemed to make Sarah McKenzie nervous, although for the life of him he couldn't figure out what he'd done to her.

The last time he'd seen her had been nearly a month

ago at his brother Matt's wedding to Dylan's mother, Ellie. At the reception the schoolteacher hadn't moved from the corner for most of the evening. In a pale peach dress and with all that sun-streaked blond hair piled on top of her head, she'd looked cool and remote and scrumptious enough to gobble up in one bite.

When he'd finally decided to ignore her blatant back-off signals and asked her to dance, she'd stared at him as if he had just dumped a glass of champagne all over her, then topped it off by stomping on her fingers.

She hadn't said anything for several painfully long moments, then she had jumped to her feet and stammered some excuse about how she needed to check on something. Next thing he'd known, he'd seen her driving out of the church parking lot as if she was trying to outgun a tornado.

He pushed the memory away. So the pretty, enigmatic Ms. McKenzie didn't want to dance with him. So what? He was a big boy now and could handle a little rejection once in a while. His little sister, Cassidy, probably would have said it was good for him.

Not that any of that had a thing to do with the reason she was sitting in front of him trying not to wring her hands together nervously.

"Is there something I can help you with, Ms. McKenzie?" he asked again, in his best casual, friendly-policeman voice.

She drew in a breath, then let it out in a rush. "I want you to arrest someone."

It was the last thing he expected her to say. "You do?"

Her soft, pretty mouth tightened. "Well, I'd prefer if you could drag him behind a horse for a few hundred miles. But since I don't think that's very likely to happen, given civil rights and all, I suppose I'll have to settle for seeing the miserable excuse for a man locked away for the rest of his natural life."

"Does this miserable excuse for a man have a name?"

She hesitated for just a few beats, just long enough to nudge his curiosity up to fever pitch. "Yes," she finally said coolly. "Yes, he does have a name. Seth Garrett."

His jaw dropped. "The mayor? You want me to arrest the mayor?"

"I don't care if he's the president of the United States. He belongs in jail."

He leaned back in his chair. "Care to tell me why, before I rush over there with my handcuffs? I'm not saying I won't do it—I'd just like to be able to give the man a reason."

She stood up, her hands clenched tightly into fists and a glare on those delicate, fine-boned features. "This is not a laughing matter, Chief Harte. If you refuse to take me seriously, I'll…I'll find someone who will. The FBI, maybe, or the Wyoming State Police."

She was serious! She wanted him to march into the mayor's office and haul him off to jail. What could she possibly have against Seth Garrett, one of the most well liked and respected men in town? He doubted the man even jaywalked.

Still, he knew she wouldn't have come here without a reason, and it was his job to listen to it. "I'm sorry, ma'am. You just took me by surprise, that's all. I didn't mean to make light of this. Sit down. What do you think he's done?"

Sarah slid into the chair again and knotted her hands

together tightly. She wasn't sure what was more to blame for their trembling—this seething fury writhing around inside her or the sick lump in her stomach at having to face the man in front of her.

She *did* know she shouldn't have come here. Jesse Harte made her so blasted nervous she couldn't think straight, and she had known before she even walked into his office that she would make a mess of this.

In the past eighteen months she had worked hard to overcome the lingering fragments of nightmare that haunted her. She wanted to think she had become almost functional again, hiding the worst of her panic attacks behind a veneer of control.

But for some reason Jesse Harte always seemed to punch a hole in the paper-thin wall of that facade, leaving her nervous and upset.

It wasn't him, exactly. Or, at least, she didn't think so. He seemed gentle enough with the girls. It was kind of sweet, actually, to see such a hard-edged cop teasing giggles out of two ten-year-old girls.

For a month she hadn't been able to shake the image of him in his dark Western-cut suit at his brother's wedding, dancing with each of the girls in turn and looking big and solid and completely masculine.

That was most of what made her nervous. He was just so big. So completely, wholly male—intimidating just by his very size and by the aura of danger that surrounded him.

With the combination of that dark-as-sin hair, those startling blue eyes and that wicked smile, Jesse Harte drew the lustful eye of every woman in town. If it weren't for the badge on his tan denim shirt, it would be difficult to remember he was on the right side of the law. All he needed was a bushy mustache and a low-slung gun belt hanging on his hips to look like the outlaw she heard he was named for.

He sent her nerves skittering just by looking at her out of those blue eyes and she hated it, but she had no one else to turn to. She had a child to protect, and if that meant facing her own personal bogeyman, she would force herself to do it, no matter the cost.

Besides her unease around the police chief, it didn't help her nerves to know she could be risking her job. When she had taken her concerns to the principal, Chuck Hendricks had ordered her to leave well enough alone. She was imagining things, he said, making problems for herself where she didn't need to.

It was a grim reminder of what had happened in Chicago. She had been warned then about stepping in where she had no business. But then, just as now, she hadn't had a choice.

"Can I get you a glass of water or something?"

She blinked and realized the police chief was waiting for some kind of an explanation for her presence here. "No. No, thank you. I'm fine."

"You ready to talk now?"

She took a deep breath, then met his gaze directly for the first time since she'd entered his office. "Mr. Garrett's stepson is in my class."

"Corey Sylvester?"

"I take it you know him."

Despite her worries over Corey, that blasted smile of his sent her stomach fluttering. "This is a small town, Ms. McKenzie. Not much slips by the eagle eye of the Salt River P.D. What's Corey done now?"

"Oh, no. He hasn't done anything."

He chuckled wryly. "That's a first."

"What do you mean?"

"Only that the boy's had his share of run-ins with local authorities."

Another person might have asked what possible crimes a child of ten could have committed to bring him to the attention of the local police chief. Not Sarah. She had seen much, much worse than Corey Sylvester could even contemplate. In Chicago, children as young as eight dealt drugs and sold their bodies on street corners and murdered each other for sport.

She thought of a pretty girl with glossy braids and old, tired eyes, then pushed the memory aside.

This was rural Wyoming, where children still played kick-the-can on a warm spring night and the most excitement to be found was at the high school baseball diamond.

That's why she had come here, to find peace. To immerse herself in the slow, serene pace of small-town life.

To heal.

"Corey has done nothing," she assured the police chief. "He's a troubled young boy and I...I believe I know why."

"I'm assuming this has something to do with his stepfather, otherwise you wouldn't be here looking for the mayor's head on a platter, right?"

Her jaw clenched as she remembered what she'd seen at school that day. "Corey has all the characteristics of an abused child. I believe his stepfather is the one abusing him."

Chief Harte leaned forward, suddenly alert as an alpha wolf scenting danger. She started to shrink back in her chair, but quickly checked the movement. She wouldn't cower. Not if she could help it.

"That's a very serious allegation, Ms. McKenzie. You have any evidence to back that up?"

She felt sick all over again just thinking about it. "Corey's been in my class for two weeks now and—"

He interrupted her with a frown. "Only two weeks? School's out in another month. Why would he transfer into your class so late in the year when the session's almost over?"

Because he'd gone through all three of the other fourth-grade teachers and each one refused to allow him back into her class. She was his last stop on the road before expulsion.

"He had some difficulties with the other teachers. But that doesn't matter. What concerns me is that in those two weeks he has come to school twice with black eyes and once with stitches in the corner of his mouth. That's just not normal wear and tear for a boy his age."

"Corey's not like most boys."

"He's certainly a little high-strung, but he's still a child."

After a moment of studying her out of those vivid blue eyes, the police chief pulled a notebook from his pocket and began writing in it. "Two black eyes and stitches in his mouth. That's what you said, right?"

She nodded. "When I asked him about his first injury, he became extremely evasive. He refused to look me in the eye and mumbled some obviously fictitious story about falling off his bike. His second black eye came from falling out of a tree, he said."

"And the stitches?"

"Yet another fall off his bike. He said he did a face plant on the concrete."

"It's possible he's telling the truth. Maybe he's just

accident-prone. When I was a kid, I once spent a whole summer at the clinic in town getting patched up from one accident or another.''

She had a disturbing mental image of a dark-haired little boy with those blue eyes and the devil in his grin, but she quickly pushed it away.

''Corey is a rough-and-tumble kind of kid, Ms. McKenzie,'' the chief continued. ''It's only natural that he'll suffer a few scrapes and bruises along the way.''

''But four serious accidents in two weeks? Doesn't that stretch the bounds of credibility a little even for you, Chief Harte?''

He checked his notebook. ''Four? You only mentioned three.''

''I was getting to that. Today, during our last recess of the day, he ripped his shirt on the playground fence. He refused to let me help him, but through the tear in his shirt I saw what looked like bruises on his shoulder.''

''Bruises?''

''Like from a man's hand squeezing viciously hard.'' She didn't add that she'd once had similar bruises. And that even though they had faded more than a year ago, she could sometimes still feel them.

He blew out a breath, and for the first time she began to think maybe she wasn't fighting a losing battle. He scribbled a few more notes in his book, then glanced at her again. ''What makes you suspect the mayor is behind all of this?''

''When Corey transferred into my class, I examined his school records so I could be familiar with his situation. Until midway through the second grade, Corey's teachers all loved him and he had wonderful grades. The comments in his report cards were things like 'always willing to help others.' 'A joy to have in class.' 'Creative and imaginative.'"

"He's imaginative, all right. Last winter during a cold spell he poured water in the keyhole of every store on Main Street so the locks would freeze. Took us half a day to thaw everything out."

"His behavior in class began to change dramatically, coinciding quite noticeably around the time I understand his mother married Mayor Garrett. Almost overnight, a bright, artistic child turned angry and destructive. I believe there's a connection."

"A lot of kids have trouble adjusting to divorces and remarriages. Doesn't mean they're being abused."

She glared at him, feeling as if she'd lost all the headway she thought she'd gained. Why wasn't he taking this seriously? She had been through this for more than an hour with Principal Hendricks and she had had just about enough of Salt River's good-old-boy network. She had no doubt that's why she seemed to be hitting a brick wall here. Nobody wanted to rock the boat, especially when powerful people were on board.

"Do you care about this child's welfare at all? Or is he just one more juvenile delinquent to you?"

He blinked at her sudden attack. "Sure I care about him. But I just can't jump into a major investigation based on speculation and conjecture."

Speculation and conjecture? She'd given him ample cause to investigate. Wasn't he listening to her at all?

Furious, she glared at him, completely forgetting that the man was supposed to intimidate her. "You mean you don't want to alienate the mayor by pursuing an investigation against him. Isn't that right?"

She narrowed her gaze thoughtfully. "That's it, isn't it? I think I'm beginning to understand. Seth Garrett is an important man around here. Tell me, Chief Harte, are you more concerned about keeping your job or in protecting a little boy?''

As soon as the words escaped her tongue, she knew they were a mistake. A monumental mistake. The police chief's blue eyes hardened. His easy charm disappeared, leaving only raw anger.

''Be careful, ma'am,'' he murmured.

She clasped her hands together tightly in her lap to hide their renewed trembling. Where had that outburst of hers come from?

The old Sarah might have said something exactly like that, would have faced down a hundred Jesse Hartes if she had to. But she had been gone for a long time. The timid mouse she had left behind never would have risked baiting a man like him.

Some vestige of her former self must have been lurking inside her all this time. What's more, she was amazed to suddenly discover she wasn't willing to run away just because of his threat, implied or otherwise. Corey deserved to have someone on his side.

Even if that someone was only a timid mouse.

She stood up again. ''If you're not willing to investigate, I told you, I'll find someone who is.''

After a moment's hesitation, he stood, as well. ''I didn't say I wasn't going to investigate. I'll look into the matter. I'll talk to the boy, talk to Seth and Ginny. But I have to warn you, I'm not sure how far I'll get. These cases can be difficult to prove, especially if the child won't cooperate. And knowing Corey, I can pretty much guess how it will go.''

''Please let me know what happens.'' She walked toward the door.

"Oh, I'll be in touch, Ms. McKenzie," the police chief said. "You can be sure of that."

That's exactly what she was afraid of, Sarah thought as she walked out of his office.

Chapter 2

It was nearly six when Jesse pulled into the Garretts' driveway. He climbed out of the department Bronco and gazed up at the house, all three stories of it.

Somebody had been busy with spring cleaning, judging by the way the windows gleamed gold in the dying sun, without a streak. The place radiated warmth and elegance, from its perfectly manicured gardens to its cobblestone sidewalk.

The house was only a few years old, but a lifetime away from the miserable one-bedroom trailer halfway up Elk Mountain where Ginny and Corey had lived during her marriage to Hob Sylvester.

Jesse had worked for the county then as a deputy sheriff and he'd always hated going out on domestic disturbance calls there. He could still remember the tangible feeling of despair that permeated the thin, painfully bare walls, and his constant, frustrating attempts to convince Ginny to get out of the situation.

Oh, she would try. He knew that. She would move
out for a few days or a week or two. But Hob still had
enough high school football star in him to sweet-talk
her back.

Hob hadn't always been a son of a bitch, and maybe
that was one of the things that kept Ginny hanging on.
Once he'd been all charisma and slow, cowboy charm,
the high school football standout everybody pegged to
go pro. It hadn't worked out that way. Something went
wrong—Jesse wasn't sure what—and a few years later
Ginny got pregnant.

Jesse figured Hob must have seen it as just one more
dirty trick played on him by fate. He'd done the right
thing by marrying her, or what was considered the right
thing by society, anyway. It sure as hell hadn't been
the right thing for Ginny. Hob had spent the next six
years drinking hard and taking his bitterness out on her.

For more than a few of those years, Jesse had been
just like him. It was a chapter in his life he hated to
even remember, how after his parents' deaths he'd
spent many a night at the Renegade, trying to drown
his guilt any way he could.

Jesse pushed the memory away. Anyway, Hob was
gone. He'd taken up with a cocktail waitress from
Idaho Falls about four years ago and the two of them
had headed for Vegas, last Jesse heard.

Ginny had landed on her feet, that's for sure. Ended
up marrying her divorce attorney and now she and her
kid lived in one of the fanciest houses in town and she
drove a Range Rover and shopped at all the ritzy designer stores in Jackson Hole.

He thought of Sarah McKenzie's accusations. He really hoped she was wrong. Ginny deserved a happy
ending, after what she'd been through.

As he walked up the front steps, the intoxicating smells of spring drifted around him—sweet lilac bushes, damp, musty earth and meat sizzling on somebody's grill nearby.

Salt River was his town and he was fiercely protective of it. When he was a kid, he couldn't wait to get out. He'd been stupid enough to think the slow pace of a small town was strangling the life out of him. Once in a while he still hungered for something more than ticketing jaywalkers and breaking up the occasional bar fight, but he owed a debt to the people of this town.

One he'd be a long time repaying.

Besides, he couldn't imagine living anywhere else on a beautiful, warm spring night like this. It was just about perfect, with kids jumping on a trampoline down the street, people working in their yards or reading the paper on their front porches, and sprinklers thumping happily all across town.

Not *quite* perfect, he amended. He still had the matter of Sarah McKenzie's suspicions about Corey Sylvester to contend with.

He rang the doorbell and had to wait only a few seconds before Ginny Garrett answered.

Her face still retained most of the beauty that had won her the prom queen tiara in school. It brightened when she saw him, but her expression just as quickly grew wary. "What has Corey done now?" she asked, her voice resigned.

"Nothing. Least, nothing that I know about yet. That's not why I'm here, anyway."

"Oh. Well then, Seth's not home, I'm afraid. He had a late meeting with a client."

"Actually, I wanted to speak with you."

Again, wariness vied with curiosity in her expression. "Come in, then," she finally said. "We can talk in the living room."

She led the way through the big house. Jesse had been there plenty of times on business with the mayor, but he always felt out of place amid the creamy whites and fancy furniture—afraid to move wrong in case he broke something expensive.

"Where's Maddie?" he asked, of Corey's six-month-old half sister.

"Napping. Finally." Ginny rolled her eyes. "I know it's almost bedtime anyway, but it's been one of those days. She's teething and has been running me ragged today. Would you care for something to drink? A pop or something?"

"No. I'm fine. I'd just as soon get this over with."

She glanced at him. "That sounds pretty ominous. What's this about, Jess?"

He sighed heavily. Damn, he didn't want to do this. Ginny had been his friend for a long time—the first girl he'd ever kissed, way back in the second grade.

After the car accident that had killed his parents and left him in the hospital for nearly a month, she'd been one of the few people who didn't offer him empty platitudes. Or, worse, who acted as if nothing had happened, when his whole life had just been ripped apart.

She had offered simple, calming comfort and he had never forgotten it.

Since then, she'd been to hell and back and had worked hard to make something out of her life. How could he tell her about Ms. McKenzie's suspicions?

"Come on, Jess. Out with it. You're scaring me."

He blew out a breath, then met her worried gaze squarely. "How do Corey and Seth get on?"

Her brow furrowed. "What kind of question is that? They get along fine."

"All the time?"

She continued to look puzzled. "Certainly they have their differences, I suppose. Corey can be difficult sometimes and he has a hard time with authority—you should know that as well as anybody. But Seth tries hard to be a good father. Why do you ask?"

Damn, this was tough. "There's been an allegation that Corey is being abused."

She stared at him, the color draining from her face until her skin just about matched the white of the sofa she was sitting on. "Abused? By Seth?"

He nodded grimly.

"This is some kind of sick joke, right? Who would say such a terrible thing? It's not true. Absolutely not true."

"It's not completely unfounded, Gin. I understand he's had several injuries in the last few weeks."

"He's a boy. A boy who gets into more than his fair share of mischief, but still just a boy. He has accidents."

"You have to admit, it looks pretty suspicious, that many injuries in such a short period of time."

"No. You're wrong." She jumped up and began to pace around the room. "Who is saying such terrible things? Who would want to hurt us like this?"

For a moment he debated telling her it was Sarah McKenzie, then he discarded the idea. Sarah still had to teach Corey in her class for the rest of the school year and he didn't want to stir up trouble for her where he didn't need to. "At this point, let's just say it's a concerned citizen. I swear, it's no one with a hidden agenda, just somebody who cares about your son's welfare.''

"Well, they're wrong. Dead wrong."

Sometimes he really hated this job. "I'm sorry, but I have to ask you, Ginny. Have you ever seen Seth hurting your son or do you have any reason to believe he might do so when you're not around?"

Her mouth compressed into a thin line. She was quiet for several long moments. When she finally spoke, her voice was low and hurt. "How can you even think such a thing, Jess? You, of all people, should know better. You know what it was like for us before. Do you honestly think, after what my son has been through, that I would stand by and do nothing while it happens all over again?"

He believed her. How could he do anything else, faced with such complete, passionate sincerity?

"Seth is a good man," she went on. "He's decent and caring and in the last two years he's been a wonderful father to Corey. He loves him, just as much as he loves Maddie. He even wants to adopt him!"

He sat back. "I'm sorry, Ginny. I had a hard time believing it, too, but I had to follow through and investigate."

"I understand."

"Did Corey have an explanation for being so accident-prone lately?"

Before she could answer, the front door opened and they heard the chink of keys being placed on a table in the hall.

Ginny paled a shade lighter. "That will be Seth. This is going to kill him, to have someone accuse him of such a thing."

"Ginny?" the mayor called from the entry. "Why

is a police Bronco parked in the driveway?'' A moment later, he poked his head into the living room. He frowned when he saw Jess. ''Chief! Is something wrong?''

''Seth, you'd better sit down,'' Ginny began.

With a puzzled frown the mayor took a seat next to her. After Jesse reluctantly explained the purpose for his visit, Seth appeared just as shocked as his wife.

''It's absolutely not true,'' he said vehemently. ''You must know that. I would never lay a hand on the boy.''

''I had to investigate, Seth.''

''Of course you did.'' He frowned. ''It must have taken great courage for someone to step forward with those kinds of suspicions. Too many people just look the other way, not wanting to get involved. I'd like to know who instigated this.''

Again Jesse thought of Sarah McKenzie and her nervousness in his office. He found himself strangely reluctant to mention her involvement, again using the excuse that she still had to teach Corey for the rest of the school year and it might make things awkward for her.

Rather than answer Seth, he opted to change the subject instead. ''Something is still going on with Corey and I think we need to find out what. That many accidents in such a short time is pretty suspicious. Do you think someone else might be hurting him?''

Ginny looked as if she might be sick. Seth must have seen it, too. He grabbed her hand and squeezed tightly. ''Who?'' he asked. ''Who would do that?''

''I don't know. Maybe someone at school. Has Corey given you any reason to think he's being bullied? Or that he's been fighting with any of the other boys?''

"If anyone is beating on him, it's probably that Connor boy." Seth's voice dripped disgust.

"Luke's kid?"

Ginny nodded. "He's always hanging around with Corey. But he's in junior high school! What does he want with a ten-year-old?"

Dusty Connor had been in just as many scrapes with the law as Corey. Where Corey's shenanigans leaned toward the clever and mischievous, Dusty's were usually plain mean.

"I don't know, but I think we need to find out," Jesse said.

"How?"

Before he could answer her, they heard the sound of a door slamming, then a voice from the kitchen of the house. "Mom, I'm home," Corey called.

"We're in the living room," Ginny answered. "Come in here, please."

They heard a loud, exasperated sigh and then Corey wandered into the room. With a basketball under his arm and dressed in baggy shorts, a T-shirt and high-top sneakers, he looked like most of the other ten-year-olds in town except for a black eye and all that attitude radiating from him like heat waves off a sidewalk.

"What's for din—" he started to ask, then his gaze landed on Jess. For one brief instant, pure panic flickered across his expression, but he quickly hid it behind belligerence. "I didn't do nothin'."

Interesting. Now, why would the kid suddenly break a sweat just at the sight of a cop when he'd always been a cocky little wise guy, even when Jesse or one of the five officers in his department caught him red-handed up to something?

What was he messed up in now that had him so jumpy? Whatever it was, Jesse had a bad feeling about it. He obviously needed to keep a better eye on the kid.

He raised an eyebrow. "What makes you so sure you're in trouble?"

"I'm not?" Corey's voice cracked on the second word.

"Should you be?"

"No. I told you, I ain't done nothin'."

"Haven't done anything," Ginny corrected quietly.

"Whatever."

"Good," Jesse said, thinking fast. "Because I need your help."

All three of them stared at him. To Ginny and Seth, he sent a reassuring smile. He'd been a cop a long time and the one thing he'd learned was to trust his instincts. He could start interrogating the boy about his injuries—the black eyes, the cut, whatever bruises the schoolteacher had seen that afternoon.

But judging by his experiences with Corey, he was sure the kid wouldn't tell them a thing. He would turn closemouthed and uncooperative and give Jesse the same bull he'd been giving everybody else about his injuries.

On the other hand, if he could spend a little time with Corey—convince the kid to trust him—maybe Jesse could get to the bottom of this.

"I'm in need of a partner for a couple days. You interested?"

The boy looked baffled. "A partner?"

"Yeah. I'm coming to school next month to talk about crime prevention." That much was true, at least.

The annual visit had been scheduled for weeks. The rest he was making up as he went along.

"I was thinking I could use somebody who knows his way around to help me out," Jesse went on. "Give the other kids some pointers about how to stay safe and out of trouble."

"Me? You want *me* to help you?"

"Why not?"

The boy looked as if he could think of a million reasons why not, but there was also an unmistakable curious light in his eyes.

Jesse decided to play on that. "You don't have to do it if you don't want to, but I could really use your help. If you agree to help me, you'll need to come to the station a few times so we can figure out what we're going to do. What do you think?"

"Sounds lame."

"Maybe. That's why I need your help. You can make me sound cool enough that the kids will listen to me."

"You want me to help you be *cool?*"

He had to fight a triumphant grin at the unwilling fascination in the boy's eyes at the idea. "Yeah. Think you can handle it?"

"I don't know, Chief." The kid sent him a sidelong look. "Could be a pretty tough job."

Jesse laughed. "I think you're man enough to handle it."

Corey chewed his lip, and Jesse could just about see the wheels turning in his head as he tried to figure out all the angles. He held his breath, waiting for the boy's answer. After a few beats, Corey shrugged his bony shoulders. "Sure. Why not?"

"Great. Meet me at my office tomorrow after school."

"Whatever. Can I go now?" he asked his mother.

Ginny nodded. As soon as they heard footsteps pounding up the stairs, both of the Garretts turned to him.

"What was that all about?" Seth asked.

"It was a spur-of-the-moment thing. I figured maybe if I have a chance to talk one-on-one with him, he might open up a little and tell me what's going on."

"Are you sure Corey would be willing to do this?" Ginny asked with a frown. "And even if he does, how do you know he'll talk to you?"

"Well, even if he doesn't open up and talk to me about whatever's going on with him, maybe he'll learn something himself about staying out of trouble."

A strident cry echoed through the house suddenly. "There's Maddie." Ginny rose from the couch.

Jesse stood, as well. "I'll get out of your hair, then."

"Would you like to stay for supper? We're having fried chicken and mashed potatoes."

The offer of some decent home cooking for a change had his mouth watering.

He used to drop by the family ranch two or three nights a week when Cassie lived there with Matt and Lucy. She was divine in the kitchen. But after Matt's wedding, Cassie had surprised them all by taking a job at a dude ranch north of town and moving out. Since Jesse didn't want to bug the newlyweds while they were busy setting up house, for the past month he'd had to make do with his own pitiful attempts at cooking.

As much as he wouldn't mind staying for supper, he suddenly decided he'd much rather stop in to see Sarah

McKenzie again. She was probably wondering what had happened with Corey.

And he had a powerful hankering to see if he could figure out what had put those shadows in her pretty green eyes.

Every muscle in her body ached.

That would teach her to spend two solid hours yanking weeds and hauling compost. Sarah winced at the burn in her arms as she tried to comb the snarls out of her hair. Even after a long, pounding shower with water as hot as she could stand, her muscles still cried out in protest.

She was so out of shape, it was pathetic. After the attack, she had become almost manic about trying to rebuild the damage that had been done to her body. Maybe on some subconscious level she had thought if she were stronger or faster she could protect herself. She had followed her physical therapy routine religiously, working for hours each day to regain strength.

Eventually, though, she had become so frustrated at the reality of her new, permanent limitations that she had eased off.

After she came to Salt River, it had been so exhausting at first just keeping up with her students she hadn't had energy to exercise. Eventually, she fell into a busy routine that didn't leave much time for anything but school.

Still, she should have made time. Working out in the yard shouldn't leave her knee on fire and the rest of her throbbing muscles jumbled into one big ache.

It had seemed like a good idea at the time. She thought working in the garden after school might calm her nerves, just as it always did. But she was just as edgy and upset as she had been at the police station.

By now, Chief Harte had probably spoken with the Garretts. She should be relieved, and she was. She *was.* Whoever was hurting that child deserved to be punished. She knew that and believed it fiercely. At the same time, she couldn't help the nervousness that had settled in her stomach and refused to leave, or the tiny voice that called her crazy for getting involved at all.

Hadn't she learned her lesson? Hadn't Tommy DeSilva taught her in savage, brutal detail what happened to nosy schoolteachers who didn't mind their own business?

She pushed the thought away. Once more she had a child to protect—it wasn't simply a case of turning in a vicious criminal. She had made the right decision, eighteen months ago and today. She had done what she had to do. The only thing she *could* have done.

She didn't want to think about it. Any of it. After quickly pulling her hair into a ponytail to keep it out of her face, she limped from the bedroom to the kitchen, her knee crying out with every step.

Dinner was the usual, something packaged out of the freezer and intended to be eaten in solitude. What was more pitiful than shoving a frozen dinner in the microwave, then eating it in front of the television set alone? she wondered.

She had to get out more, she thought as she finally settled on a low-fat chicken-and-rice meal. It was a vow she made to herself with grim regularity, but she never seemed to do anything about it. When was the last time she'd shared an evening meal with someone besides Tom Brokaw? She couldn't even remember.

She never used to be such an introvert. In Chicago

she'd had a wide, eclectic circle of friends. Artists, social activists, computer geeks. They went to plays and poetry readings and Cubs games together.

At first her friends had tried to rally around her, with cards and gifts and visits in the hospital. Unable to face their awkwardness and pity, she had pushed them all away, even Andrew.

Especially Andrew.

She had given him back his ring when she was still in the hospital, and he had taken it with a guilty relief that shamed both of them.

She didn't blame him. Not really. That day had changed her, had shattered something vital inside her. Eighteen months later she still hadn't made much progress repairing it.

She knew her friends and family all thought she was running away when she decided to take a teaching job in small-town Wyoming. She couldn't deny there was truth to that. She *had* been running away, had searched the Internet for job listings in small towns as far away as she could find.

But escaping Chicago and the grim memories of that fateful morning had been only part of the reason she had come here.

She needed to be in a place where she could feel clean again.

The microwave dinged. Grateful to escape her thoughts, she reached in with a pot holder to pull out her dinner just as the doorbell chimed through the little house.

She'd heard the sound so seldom that it took her a moment to figure out what it was. Who could be here? Her heart fluttered with wild panic for just an instant, but she took a quick, calming breath. She had nothing to worry about, not here in Salt River.

Setting her plate on the table, she made her way out of the kitchen and down the hall to the door, careful not to put too much stress on her knee. At first all she could see through the peephole was a hard, broad chest, but then she saw the badge over one tan denim pocket and realized it must be Chief Harte.

Her heart fluttered again, but she wasn't completely sure it was only with panic this time. Why did the man have such an effect on her? She hated it. Absolutely hated it!

The bell rang—impatiently, she thought—and with one more deep breath, she opened the door.

His smile sent her pulse into double time. "I was just driving home and thought I'd check in with you and let you know how things went at the mayor's place."

As much as she'd like to, she knew she couldn't very well talk to him through the screen door "I...come in." She held the door open, wishing she were wearing something a little more professional than a pair of faded jeans and an old Northwestern sweatshirt.

The small foyer shrank by half as soon as he walked inside. There was absolutely no way she could stand there and carry on a half-rational conversation with him looming over her, looking so big and imposing. The house she rented was tiny, with a living room only a few feet larger than the entry. Where else could they go?

"It's a nice night," she said impulsively. "We can talk outside. Is that all right?"

She took his shrug for assent and led him through

the house to the covered porch, flipping on the recessed lights overhead as they went through the door.

The back porch had become her favorite spot lately. She hadn't realized how closed in and trapped she'd been feeling during the harsh Wyoming winter until the relentless snow finally began to give way to spring.

As the temperatures warmed, she discovered she liked to sit out here in the evenings and look up at the mountains. Their massive grandeur comforted her, in some strange way she couldn't define.

A few weeks ago she'd found some wicker furniture in the shed and dragged it up the porch stairs. She'd purchased matching cushions and hung baskets overflowing with flowers around the porch to create a cozy little haven. She'd been very pleased with the results, but now, trying to see the place through Chief Harte's eyes, she felt awkward. Exposed, somehow.

He sprawled into one of the wicker chairs, completely dwarfing it. "This is nice," he murmured. "Hell of a view from here."

"I imagine you're used to it, since you grew up in Star Valley."

His mouth quirked into a half smile that did more annoying things to her nerves. "I've seen those mountains just about every day of the last thirty-three years and they still sometimes take my breath away."

She wouldn't have expected such an admission from him. It made him seem perhaps a little softer, a little less intimidating, to know they shared this, at least.

Before she could come up with an answer, he settled back into his chair and stretched his long legs out in front of him until his boots almost touched one of her sneakers. Closing his eyes, he looked for all the world as if he were settling in for the night.

"This is really nice," he repeated.

She cleared her throat, suddenly not at all sure she wanted Jesse Harte lounging so comfortably on her back porch. "So what happened at the Garretts? Did you make an arrest?"

"No. Sorry to disappoint you, but the mayor is still a free man. And it looks like he's going to stay that way."

She stared at him. "Why?"

He opened one eye. "He and Ginny both said he'd never hurt the boy, and I believe them."

"Just like that?"

"Just like that."

Renewed fury pounded through her. It had all been for nothing—risking her job and tangling with the man she had spent eight months doing her best to avoid. For nothing.

Despite her own nightmares, she had done the right thing by going to the proper authority and he had basically laughed in her face.

Calm down, Sarah.

A corner of her brain sent out strident warning bells that she was going to say or do something she would regret, but she ignored it, lost to everything but her anger.

"I can't believe this," she snapped. "If I ever wanted to commit a crime, Salt River, Wyoming, would obviously be the place for it. All I have to do is swear to the police chief that I didn't do anything and I'll be home free."

He dropped his relaxed pose as easily as a snake shedding his skin and straightened in the chair. "Now, wait a minute…"

"Of course, maybe I'd have to be a powerful person

like the mayor so I can get away with it,'' she went on, as if he hadn't spoken. ''Apparently, holding political office around here gives a person the right to do whatever he darn well pleases.''

''I can see where you'd think that, but you're wrong. Dead wrong. If I thought for one minute Seth had given that boy so much as a hangnail, you can be damn sure I wouldn't let him get away with it.''

''Lucky for him, then, that he managed to convince you he didn't do anything. I'd like you to leave now, Chief Harte.''

She whirled away from him with an angry, abrupt movement, completely forgetting that her knee was in no condition to withstand the stress of such a quick motion.

She heard an ominous pop, then she had the sudden, sick sensation of falling as her knee gave out.

One instant she was tumbling toward the hard wooden slats of the porch, the next she heard an alarmed ''Hey!'' and found herself wrapped in strong male arms, shoved back against a hard, muscled chest.

For a moment she froze as she was surrounded by heat and strength, helpless to get away. And then panic took over. *He* had held her just like this, from behind, with her arms locked at her sides.

Instantly she was once more in that dingy Chicago classroom, with its dirty windows and broken desks and stale, tired air.

Not again. She wouldn't let this happen again.

She couldn't breathe, suddenly, couldn't think. Her heart was racing, adrenaline pumping like crazy, and only one thought pierced her panic.

Escape.

Somehow, some way, this time she had to escape.

Chapter 3

What in the hell?

Jesse held an armload of kicking, fighting female and tried to figure out what had set her off like this.

All he had tried to do was keep her from hitting the ground when she started to topple. One minute she'd been standing there, her pretty mouth hard and angry as she ordered him out of her house, the next she had turned into this wild, out-of-control banshee, flailing her arms around and twisting every which way.

He figured her bum leg must have given out and that's what had made her start to fall. The way she was fighting him, she was only going to hurt it even more—and maybe something else, too.

She wanted out of his arms. He could respect that. Only problem was, if he let her go now, she would still hit the ground.

"Take it easy, ma'am," he murmured softly, sooth-

ingly, the way he would to one of Matt's skittish colts.
"It's okay. I'm only trying to help. I won't hurt you."

Carefully, moving as slowly as he could manage
with his arms full of trouble, he eased her down to the
floor. The lower to the ground they moved, though, the
more frenzied she fought him. Through the delicate
skin at her wrists he could feel her pulse trembling and
she was breathing in harsh, ragged gasps.

He finally was close enough to the wooden slats of
the porch that he could release her safely. As soon as
she was on solid ground, he moved back, crouching to
her level a few feet away. "See? No harm done."

For a moment she just stared at him, her big green
eyes dazed and lost. She blinked several times, her
small chest heaving under that soft old sweatshirt as
she tried to catch her breath.

He knew exactly when she snapped back into the
present—her eyes lost that frantic, fight-or-flight look
and a deep flush spread from her neck to her cheekbones like bright red paint spilling across canvas.

"I… Oh."

In those expressive eyes he could see mortification
and something deeper. Almost shame.

She cleared her throat and shifted her gaze to the
ground. "I'm so sorry." Her voice was small, tight.
"Did I hurt you?"

"Nope." He tried to smile reassuringly, for all the
good it did him, since she wouldn't look at him. "I've
run into much tougher customers than you."

"I don't doubt that," she murmured, a deep, old
bitterness in her voice.

Her hands still shook and he had to fight the urge to
reach out and cover those slender, trembling fingers
with his.

She wouldn't welcome the comfort right now. He knew she wouldn't. And she'd probably jump right through the porch roof if he obeyed his other sudden, completely irrational impulse—to reach forward and press his mouth to that wildly fluttering pulse he could see beating quickly through an artery at the base of her throat.

"You want to tell me what that was all about?" he asked instead.

She still refused to meet his gaze. "You just startled me, that's all. I don't like being startled."

Yeah, like a wild mustang doesn't like rowels dug into his sides. Eyes narrowed, he watched her for several more seconds, then realized she wasn't going to tell him anything more about the reason for her panic.

"How's the leg?"

"The…the leg?"

"That's what started this whole thing, remember? You turned to walk away from me and it must have given out. I tried to keep you from falling and you suddenly went off like a firecracker on the Fourth of July."

The blush spread even farther. "I'm sorry," she whispered again. "Thank you for trying to help."

She reached out and used a chair for leverage to stand, then tested her weight gingerly. "It's my knee, not my leg. It gives me trouble sometimes if I move too quickly."

Was that the reason for that slight, mysterious limp of hers? What had caused it? he wondered. An accident of some kind? The same accident that made her spirit seem so wounded, that put that wild panic in her green eyes when somebody touched her unexpectedly?

He had a thousand questions, but he knew she

wouldn't answer any of them. "Sit down. Need me to call Doc Wallace and have him come take a look at it?"

"No. I'm fine. It should be all right in a few moments."

"Can I bring you something, then? A glass of water or juice or something? A pillow, maybe, to put that leg on?"

She sat down and gave him an odd look, as if she didn't know quite what to make of the Salt River police chief trying to play nurse. "No, I told you, I'm fine. It's happened before. Usually, if I can just sit still for a few moments it will be all right."

After a moment he shrugged and sprawled into the wicker chair across from her. "In that case, you're in no condition to kick me out, so I'll just sit here with you until you're back on your feet. Just to make sure you don't need a doctor or anything."

"That's not necessary. I told you, I'll be perfectly fine."

"Humor me. It's my civic duty. Can't leave a citizen of the good town of Salt River in her hour of need. Now, where were we?" Jesse scratched his cheek. "Oh, that's right. I was telling you what happened at the mayor's."

"You mean you were telling me what *didn't* happen," she muttered. Her fiery color began to fade, he saw with satisfaction, until it just about matched those soft pink early climbing roses around her back porch that sent their heady aroma through the cool evening air.

"We covered that. What I didn't have a chance to tell you is that I think you're right. Something's definitely going on with that kid."

Her green eyes widened. "You agree with me?"

"Someone is behind all those little 'accidents' of his, but I'm not convinced it's the mayor."

"Who, then? Surely not his mother?"

He snorted. "Ginny? Hell—" he paused "—er, *heck* no."

"You don't need to guard your tongue around me, Chief Harte. I've heard a few epithets in my time. Probably some that would make even you blush."

"I doubt that. Anyone who uses words like 'epithets' couldn't have heard too many raunchy ones."

"You'd be surprised what you can hear in a school hallway."

"You teach the fourth grade," he exclaimed, appalled. "How bad could the cuss words get?"

Her lips curved slightly, but she straightened them quickly, before the unruly things could do something crazy like smile, he figured. "I didn't mean my students here, although I still certainly hear some choice language from them occasionally."

"Where, then?"

"Where what?" She shifted her gaze down again, her fingers troubling a loose thread in her jeans.

Why did she have to be so damn evasive about everything? Getting information out of the woman was as tough as trying to get those blasted climbing roses to grow in January.

"Where did you hear the kind of words that could make a rough-edged cop like me blush?"

She was a silent for a moment, and then she took a deep breath and met his gaze. "Before I came to Wyoming, I taught for five years at a school on Chicago's south side."

All he could do was stare at her. He wouldn't have

been more shocked if she'd just told him she used to be an exotic dancer.

The fragile, skittish schoolmarm who jumped if you looked at her the wrong way used to walk the rough-and-tumble hallways of an inner-city school? She had to be joking, didn't she? One look at her tightly pursed mouth told him she wasn't. Before he could press her on it, though, she quickly changed the subject.

"If you don't believe Corey's being abused, what sort of trouble do you think he's involved with?"

He barely heard, still focused on her startling disclosure. Why did she leave Chicago? Did it have anything to do with her panicky reaction to him earlier? Or with her knee that still gave her trouble if she moved the wrong way?

With frustration, he realized his burning curiosity was going to have to wait. Judging by that withdrawn look on her face, she wasn't about to satisfy it anytime soon.

He gave a mental shrug. He'd get the information out of her sooner or later. He was a cop. It was his job to solve mysteries.

"I don't know," he said, in answer to her question about Corey. "But whatever it is, I doubt it's legal. He sure looked scared when he came home and found me sitting with his parents."

"What do you plan to do next?"

"Try to find out what he's up to. I figured maybe if I can talk to him one-on-one, he might open up a little more."

"I take it you have a plan."

He nodded. "I'm coming to the grade school next month to talk about crime prevention, and he's going to be my assistant. I expect it will take us several days to get ready, which ought to give me plenty of time to find out what's been going on with him.''

''And he agreed to help you?''

''He wasn't too crazy about it at first, but he finally came around. I think it will be good for him.'' He paused. ''If someone is hurting that kid, I'll find out, Sarah. I promise you that.''

She gazed at him, green eyes wide and startled at his vehemence. Tilting her head, she studied him closely as if trying to gauge his sincerity. Whatever she saw in his expression must have satisfied her. After a few moments she offered him a smile. Not much of one, just a tentative little twitch of her lips, but it was definitely still a smile.

He felt as jubilant as if he'd just single-handedly brought every outlaw in the Wild West to justice.

''Thank you,'' Sarah murmured, her voice as soft as that spring breeze that teased her blond hair like a lover's hand.

''You're welcome,'' he answered gruffly, knowing damn well he shouldn't be so entranced by a tiny smile and a woman with secrets in her eyes.

''And I'm sorry for the terrible things I said to you,'' she went on. ''I had no right to say such things. To judge you like that.''

He had to like a woman who could apologize so sweetly. ''You're a teacher concerned about one of her students. You were willing to do what you thought was the right thing, which is more than most people would in the same situation.''

She didn't seem to take his words as the compliment he intended. Instead, her mouth tightened and she looked away from him toward the wooden slats of the porch.

What the hell had he said to make her look as if she wanted to cry? He gave an inward, frustrated sigh. Just when he thought he was making progress with her, she clammed up again.

He ought to just let it ride. Sarah McKenzie was obviously troubled by things she figured were none of his business. But something about that lost, wounded look that turned her green eyes murky brought all his protective instincts shoving their way out.

"Something wrong?" he asked.

"No," she said curtly. "Nothing at all."

"How's the knee?"

She looked disoriented for a moment, then glanced down at her outstretched leg. "Oh. I think it's feeling much better." Gripping the arms of the wicker rocker, she rose to her feet and carefully tested it with her weight. "Yes. Much better."

She was lying. He could tell by the lines of pain that bracketed her mouth like sagging fence posts.

"You sure?"

"Yes. Positive. I'm fine. I appreciate all your help, Chief Harte, but I'm sure you have better things to do than baby-sit me."

He couldn't think of a single one, especially if he stood half a chance of coaxing more than that sad little smile out of her. But she obviously wanted him gone, and his mama hadn't raised her kids to be rude. Well, except for Matt, maybe.

Anyway, he'd have another chance to see those green eyes soften and her soft, pretty mouth lift at the corners. And if an excuse to see her again didn't present itself, he'd damn well make one up.

"If you're sure you're okay, I'll leave so you can

get back to the supper I dragged you away from. It's probably cold by now.''

She grimaced. ''I'm afraid it's not much of a meal, hot or cold. A frozen dinner.''

It broke his heart to think of her sitting alone here with her solitary dinner. If he thought for a second she'd agree to go with him, he'd pack her into his Bronco and take her down to the diner for some of Murphy's turkey-fried steak.

But even though he had willingly left the ranch work to Matt, he had still gentled enough skittish mustangs in his time to know when to call it a day. He had a feeling he was going to have to move very slowly if he wanted to gain the schoolteacher's trust.

Asking her to dinner would probably send her loping away faster than the Diamond Harte's best cutter after a stray.

No hurry. He could be a patient man, when the situation called for it. He would bide his time, let her know she had nothing to fear from him.

Meanwhile, he now had two mysteries on his hands: Corey Sylvester and whatever mischief he was up to. And Sarah McKenzie.

The pretty schoolteacher had scars. Deep ones. And he wasn't about to rest until he found out who or what had given them to her.

Chapter 4

The nightmare attacked just before dawn.

She should have expected it, given the stress of the day. Seeing Corey Sylvester's bruises, the visit to the police station that had been so reminiscent of the extensive, humiliating interviews she had given in Chicago, and two encounters with the gorgeous but terrifying Jesse Harte.

It was all more than her still-battered psyche could handle.

If she had been thinking straight, she would have tried to stay up, to fight the dream off with the only tool she had—consciousness. But the sentence diagrams she was trying to grade worked together with the exhausting stress of the day to finish her off. After her fourth yawn in as many minutes, she had finally given up. She was half-asleep as she checked the locks and turned off the lights sometime around midnight.

Sleep came instantly, and the dream followed on its heels.

It was as familiar to her as her *ABC*s. Walking into her empty classroom. Humming softly to the Beethoven sonata that had been playing on her car CD. Wondering if she would be running on schedule after school to meet Andrew before the opening previews at the little art theater down the street from her apartment.

She unlocked her classroom door and found him waiting for her, his face hard and sharp and his eyes dark with fury.

She hadn't been afraid. Not at first. At first she'd only been angry. He should have been in jail, behind bars where he belonged.

The detective she had made her report to the afternoon before—O'Derry, his name had been—had called her the previous evening to let her know officers had picked up DeSilva. But he had also warned her even then that the system would probably release the eighteen-year-old on bail just a few hours later.

She knew why he had come—because she had dared step up to report him for dealing drugs and endangering the welfare of a child. She imagined he would threaten her, maybe warn her to mind her own business. She never guessed he would hurt her.

How stupid and naive she had been in her safe, middle-class world. She had taught at an inner-city school long enough that she should have realized anyone willing to use a nine-year-old girl to deliver drugs to vicious criminals would be capable of anything.

"How did you get in?" she started to ask, then saw shattered glass from the broken window all over the floor and the battered desks closest to it. How was she supposed to teach her class now with cool October air rushing in? With the stink and noise of the city oozing in along with it?

Before she could say anything more, he loomed in front of her. "You messin' with the wrong man, bitch."

Still angry about the window, she spoke without thinking. "I don't see a man here," she said rashly. "All I can see is a stupid punk who hides behind little girls."

He hissed a name then—a vicious, obscene name—and the wild rage in his features finally pierced her self-righteous indignation. For the first time, a flicker of unease crawled up her spine.

He was high on something. He might be only eighteen, but that didn't mean anything on the street. Punk or not, a furious junkie was the most dangerous creature alive.

She started to edge back toward the door, praying one of the custodians would be within earshot, but DeSilva was faster. He beat her to the door and turned the lock, then advanced on her, a small chrome handgun suddenly in his hand.

"You're not goin' anywhere," he growled.

She forced herself to stay calm. To treat him coolly and reasonably, as she would one of her troubled students. "You won't use that on me. The detectives who arrested you will know who did it. They'll arrest you within the hour."

"Maybe. But you'll still be dead."

"And the minute you fire a shot, everybody in the place is going to come running. Are you going to kill them all, too?"

He squinted, trying to follow her logic, and she saw

his hand waver slightly. Pushing her advantage, she held out her own hand. "Come on. Give me the gun."

For several long moments he stared at her, a dazed look on his face as if he couldn't quite figure out what he was doing there. Finally, when she began to feel light-headed from fear, he shoved the gun back into his waistband and stood there shaking a little.

"Good. Okay," she murmured. "Why don't you sit down and I'll get you a glass of water?" *And maybe slip out and call the police while I'm at it,* she thought.

"I don't want a glass of water," he snarled, and without warning he smacked her hard across the face.

The force and the shock of it sent her to her knees. The next thing she knew, he had gone crazy, striking out at her with anything he could reach—the legs of her wooden chair, the stapler off her desk, the stick she used to point out locations on the map during geography.

She curled into a protective ball, but still he hit her back, her head, her legs, muttering all the while. "You have to pay. Nobody narcs on Tommy D and gets away with it. You have to pay."

A particularly hard hit at her temple from the large, pretty polished stone she used as a paperweight had her head spinning. She almost slipped into blessed unconsciousness. Oblivion hovered just out of reach, like a mirage in the desert. Before she could reach it, his mood changed and she felt the horrible weight of his hands on her breasts, moving up her thighs under her skirt, ripping at her nylons.

She fought fiercely, kicking out, crying, screaming, but as always, she was helpless to get away.

This time, before that final, dehumanizing act of bru-

tality, the school bell pealed through the dingy classroom and she was able to claw her way out of sleep.

The ringing went on and on, echoing in her ears,
until she realized it was her alarm clock.

She fumbled to turn it off, then had to press a hand
to her rolling, pitching stomach. The jarring shift between nightmare and reality always left her nauseated.
She lurched to her feet and stumbled to the bathroom,
where she tossed what was left of her dinner from the
night before.

After she rinsed her mouth, she gazed at herself in
the mirror above the sink. She hardly recognized the
pale woman who stared back at her with huge, haunted
green eyes underlined by dark purplish smears. Who
was this stranger? This fearful person who had invaded
her skin, her bones, her soul?

Gazing in the mirror, she saw new lines around her
mouth, a bleakness in her eyes. She looked more hungover than anything else, and Sarah despised the
stranger inside her all over again.

She hated the woman she had become.

For the past eighteen months she had felt as if she
were dog-paddling in some frigid, ice-choked sea, unable to go forward, unable to climb out, just stuck there
in one place while arctic waters froze the life out of
her inch by inch.

How long? How long would she let a vicious act of
violence rule her life? She pictured herself a year from
now, five years, ten. Still suffering nightmares, still hiding from the world, burying herself in her work and
her garden and her students.

She had to be stronger. She *could* be stronger.
Hadn't she proved it to some degree by going to Chief
Harte the day before with her concerns about Corey?

She couldn't consider it monumental by any stretch of the imagination. Still, she had done something, even if it was only to kick just a little harder in her frozen prison.

Beginning today, things would be different. She would *make* them different.

If she didn't, she knew it was only a matter of time before she would stop paddling completely and let herself slip quietly into the icy depths.

Her resolve lasted until she arrived at school and found Jesse Harte's police Bronco out front.

She cringed, remembering how she had fought and kicked at him the day before in the middle of another of those nasty flashbacks. He must think she was completely insane, the kind of woman who boiled pet rabbits for kicks.

Maybe she wouldn't even see him.

Maybe the vehicle belonged to a totally different officer.

Maybe an earthquake would hit just as she reached the doors to the school and she wouldn't be able to go in.

No such luck. Inside, she found Jesse standing in the glass-walled office taking notes while Chuck Hendricks—the principal of the school and the bane of her and every other Salt River Elementary teacher's existence—gestured wildly.

Whatever they were talking about wasn't sitting well with Chuck, judging by his red face and the taut veins in his neck that stood out like support ropes on a circus tent.

Jesse didn't see her, she saw with relief. She should have hurried on to her classroom, but the temptation to watch him was irresistible. The man was like some kind of dark angel. Lean and rugged and gorgeous, with rough-hewn features and those unbelievably blue eyes.

She pressed a hand to her stomach, to the funny little ache there, like a dozen tiny, fluttering birds.

"He's yummy, isn't he?"

Coloring fiercely, Sarah jerked her gaze away as if she'd been caught watching a porn movie. She had been so engrossed in watching Jesse that she hadn't even heard Janie Parker walk up and join her.

"Who?" she asked with what she sincerely hoped was innocence in her tone.

The art teacher grinned, showing off her dimples. "Salt River's favorite bad-boy cop. Jesse Harte. The man makes me want to run a few stop signs just so he'll pull me over. He can write me all the tickets he wants as long as I can drool over him while he's doing it."

Janie was probably exactly his type. Petite and curvy and cute, with a personality to match. Sarah had a quick mental picture of the two of them together, of Jesse looking down at the vivacious teacher with laughter in those blue eyes, just before he lowered that hard mouth to hers.

The image shouldn't depress her so much. She quickly changed the subject. "What's got Chuck's toupee in such a twist?" she asked.

It was exactly the kind of thing the Before Sarah would have said, something glib and light and casual. But it was obvious from Janie's raised eyebrows that she didn't expect anything remotely glib from the stiff, solemn woman Sarah had become.

The rest of the faculty must think she had no sense

of humor whatsoever. How could she blame them, when she had given them little indication of it?

She also hadn't tried very hard to make friends. Not that she hadn't wanted friends—or, heaven knows, needed them—but for the first time in her life, she hadn't been able to work up the energy.

This was one of the things she could change, if it wasn't too late. Starting today, she would go out of her way to be friendly to her fellow teachers. If anybody dared invite her anywhere after she had spent six months rebuffing all their efforts, she wouldn't refuse this time.

"Somebody broke in to the school last night," Janie finally answered.

Sarah immediately regretted her glibness. "Was it vandals?"

"Nothing was damaged as far as anybody can tell, but they got away with the Mile High Quarter Jar."

She suddenly realized that was the reason the foyer in front of the office looked different. Empty. "How? That thing must have weighed a ton!"

As a schoolwide project, the students were collecting money for the regional children's medical center and were trying to raise enough quarters to cover a mile if they were laid in a straight line.

They still had a way to go, but had raised nearly fifteen hundred dollars in quarters.

Janie shrugged. "Either we've had a visit from a superhero-turned-bad or they must have used a dolly of some kind."

"How did they get in?"

"A broken window in Chuck's office. That's probably why he's so upset. Forget the kids' money, but if he knows what's good for him, Chief Harte darn well

better catch the villains who dared scatter glass all over
His Holiness's desk.''

Broken glass littering a desk like shards of ice.

Sarah drew a quick breath and pushed the memory
aside. She forced a laugh, which earned her another
surprised look from the other teacher.

Jesse couldn't have heard it inside the office, but he
lifted his head anyway.

His gaze locked onto hers and a slow, private smile
spread over his features like the sun rising over the Salt
River range.

A simple smile shouldn't have the power to make
her blush, but she could feel more color seeping into
her cheeks. Still, she managed to give him a hesitant
smile in return, then quickly turned away to find Janie
watching the interaction with avid interest.

''Whoa. What was that all about?''

Sarah blushed harder. ''What?''

''Is there something I should know about going on
between you and our hunky police chief?''

''No. Of course not! I barely know the man.''

''So why is your face more red than Principal
Chuck's right now? Come on. Tell all!''

''There's nothing to tell.'' Without realizing it, she
used the same curt tone she would with an unruly student. ''Excuse me. I have to get to class.''

Janie's tentative friendliness disappeared and she
donned a cool mask. ''Sorry for prying.''

Sarah felt a pang as she watched it disappear. She
remembered her vow to make new friends and realized
she was blowing it, big time. ''Janie, I'm sorry. But
really, nothing's going on. Chief Harte is just…we're
just…''

"You don't have to explain. It's none of my business."

"Honestly, there's nothing to explain. I just always seem to act like an idiot around him," she confessed.

"Don't we all, sweetheart? What is it about big, gorgeous men that zaps our brain cells?"

The warmth had returned to Janie's expression, Sarah saw with relief. She wanted to bask in it like a cat sprawled out in a sunbeam.

But she knew she would have to work harder to make a new friend than just a quick conversation in the hallway. Gathering her nerve, she smiled at the other teacher. "Are you on lunch duty this week?"

"No. I had my turn last week."

"Would you like to escape the school grounds for a half hour and grab a quick bite sometime?"

If she was shocked by the invitation, Janie quickly recovered. "Sure. Just name the day."

"How about Friday?"

"Sounds perfect."

It was a start, Sarah thought as she walked to her classroom. And somehow, for just a moment, the water surrounding her didn't seem quite as cold.

Jesse tuned out Up-Chuck Hendricks and watched Sarah make her slow way down the hall toward her classroom. She was still favoring her leg, he saw with concern. Her walk was just a little uneven, like a wagon rolling along with a wobbly wheel.

He shouldn't have taken her word that everything was okay the night before. He should have insisted on hauling her to the clinic, just to check things out.

What else was he supposed to have done? He couldn't force her to go to the doctor if she didn't want to. He'd done what he could, sat with her as long as she would let him.

It amazed him how protective he felt toward her. Amazed him and made him a little uneasy. He tried to tell himself it was just a natural—if chauvinistic—re-action of a man in the presence of a soft, quiet, fragile woman. But deep down he knew it was more than that. For some strange reason he was fascinated by Sarah McKenzie, and had been since the day she moved to Star Valley.

He'd dreamed about her the night before.

He imagined she would be horror-struck if she knew the hot, steamy activities his subconscious had con-jured up for them to do together. Hell, even *he* was horror-struck when he woke up and found himself hard and ready for action. She wasn't at all his type. So why couldn't he seem to stop thinking about her?

"Are you listening to me?"

"Sure." He snapped his attention back to Chuck Hendricks, chagrined that he'd let himself get so dis-tracted from the investigation by the soft, pretty Sarah McKenzie.

He also didn't like the fact that the principal could make him feel as if he had somehow traveled twenty years back in time and was once more the troublemaker du jour in Up-Chuck's sixth-grade class.

"What are you going to do to get to the bottom of this?" Hendricks snapped. "These criminals must be caught and punished severely. I can tell you right where to start. Corey Sylvester."

The principal said the name with such seething an-imosity that a wave of sympathy for the kid washed through Jesse. He knew all too well what it was like to be at the top of Chuck's scapegoat list.

"Why Corey?" he asked.

"It's exactly the sort of thing he would do. After thirty-five years of teaching hooligans, I know a bad apple and I can tell you that boy is just plain rotten."

The principal didn't seem to notice the sudden frown and narrowed gaze of one of those former hooligans. "Besides that," he went on, "I saw him hanging around by the jar yesterday before lunch recess. It's the second or third time I've seen him there. I know he was up to no good."

"Maybe he was putting some quarters in."

Hendricks harrumphed as if the idea was the most ridiculous thing he'd ever heard. "I doubt it."

Jesse felt a muscle twitch in his jaw. He would have liked to tell Up-Chuck exactly what he thought of him, but he knew that wouldn't help him solve the case of the missing quarters. "I'll talk to him. But I've got to tell you, my instincts are telling me you're on the wrong track. I don't think he did it. Or if he did, he couldn't have acted alone."

"Why not?"

"Do the math, Chuck." His smile would have curdled milk, but his former teacher didn't seem to notice. "Corey weighs no more than sixty-five pounds. A jar with six thousand quarters would weigh a whole lot more than that. He wouldn't even be able to wrestle it onto a dolly by himself, let alone push the thing out of the building."

He paused to give the information time to sink through Hendricks's thick skull. "Then you have the matter of getting it out of here. You think he could haul a dolly weighing that much all the way to his house?"

"Well, he probably had help. Most likely that troublemaking Connor kid. You'll probably find both of them spending the loot all over town on any manner of illegal—not to mention immoral—activity.''

Yeah. Paying for booze and hookers with quarters always went over real well. ''Thanks for all the leads. I'll do my best to get the money back for the kids.''

The principal sniffed. ''I sincerely hope you do.''

Jesse sighed. Having Chuck on his case over this was going to be a major pain in the keister until he found the culprits.

Chapter 5

He managed to put off talking to Corey Sylvester for nearly two hours.

Finally he had to admit that he had nobody left to interview. He had talked to the janitor and the assistant principal, to several of the faculty members and the custodial staff. He had interviewed the residents of the three houses across the street from the school to see if any of them had heard or seen anything in the night, and he had Lou notifying local merchants and banks to give him a buzz if anybody brought in an unusual number of quarters.

He had half a mind to wrap up the initial canvas right now and forget about Corey Sylvester. It stuck in his craw that he had to treat the kid like a suspect just because Chuck Hendricks had decided to peg him as that year's scapegoat.

Jesse knew how it felt to be the kid everybody looked to when trouble broke out. He knew what it was like to be blamed any time anything came missing, to be sent to the principal's office for something he didn't have a thing to do with, to know that most people figured you would never amount to much.

He knew the deep sense of injustice a ten-year-old can experience at being unjustly accused.

He loved his older brother, but he had to admit he'd been a tough act to follow in school. Matt had been every teacher's dream. The best athlete, the best student. Trustworthy, loyal and all the rest of the Boy Scout mumbo jumbo.

Jesse, on the other hand, had struggled in school. He'd been a whiz at math, but words on a page just never seemed to fit together right for him. Reading and spelling had always been torture, right on into high school. In his frustration, maybe he'd developed a bad attitude about school, but that didn't mean he'd been a bad kid.

After a while, he'd got so tired of trying and failing to measure up to Matt's example that it had seemed easier to just give up and sink to everybody's expectations.

While his parents had still been alive, he had managed to stay out of serious trouble just because he knew how his mom's face would crumple and his dad would look at him with that terrible look of disappointment. After they'd died, everything had changed and he'd become all Chuck predicted for him.

He hated having to feed the principal's stereotypes about Corey Sylvester by interviewing the kid, especially when he was trying to find out what was going on with him. But Hendricks had said he'd seen the kid by the coin jar. What kind of a cop would he be if he ignored a possible lead, just because the source of that lead was a bitter, humorless man who had no business working with children?

He had a duty to follow up, and he had worked hard the past three years to prove he was the kind of police chief who tried his best to meet his obligations.

At least he could make the interrogation as subtle as possible. And on the upside, pulling Corey out of class would give him a chance to see Sarah McKenzie again.

While he had been busy chasing down nonexistent leads to the theft, the students had descended on Salt River Elementary. Up and down the hallway he could hear the low murmur of voices in classrooms, the squeak of chalk on chalkboards, the rustling of paper.

As he passed each doorway on the way to Sarah's room, he could see teachers lecturing in the front of their classes and students bent over their work.

Walking the hallways brought memories, thick and fast, of his own school years. This was a different school than the one he'd attended. The board of education had bonded for a new building ten years earlier and demolished the crumbling old brick two-story structure to build this modern new school, with its brown brick and carpeted walls.

It might be a different building, but it smelled just as he remembered from his own school years, a jumbled mix of wet paper and paste and chalk, all mingling with the yeasty scent of baking rolls that floated out from the cafeteria.

Ms. McKenzie's classroom was the last one on the right. He smiled at the whimsical welcome sign over her door, featuring a bird knocking at the door of an elaborate birdhouse.

He could hear her musical voice from inside and he paused for a moment to listen. She was talking in that soft, sexy voice about fractions. Despite the benign subject matter, her voice somehow managed to twine through his insides like some voracious vine.

How could he get so turned on by a shy school-teacher talking about fractions, in a building full of kids?

He watched her through the little square window set into her door, trying to figure out her appeal. She was soft and pretty in a pale blue short-sleeve sweater set and a floral skirt. Her sun-streaked hair was held back on the side by some kind of clip thing, but it fell long and luxurious to the center of her back, just inviting a man to bury his hands in it.

And that mouth. Full and lush and soft enough to make even a priest have to spend a few extra minutes in confession.

But she was still much too innocent for a wild, some-what-reformed troublemaker like Jesse Harte.

He clamped down hard on his unruly imagination and opened the door to her classroom.

Sarah turned toward him at the sound and her big green eyes widened. Interesting. Now, what made her cheeks turn pink and her breathing speed up a notch?

Before he could put his crack investigative skills toward figuring it out, he was attacked. Lucy and Dylan ambushed him from the left, throwing their arms around him and jabbering like two monkeys in a zoo.

They fired questions at him one after another. "Uncle Jess! What are you doing at school? How long will you be here? Can you stay and have school lunch with us? Can we use you for sharing today?"

He opened his mouth to pick one question to answer, but Ms. McKenzie beat him to it. "Girls," she interjected firmly, "I know you're excited about your uncle visiting our classroom. I'm sure it's a real treat for all of us, but you need to take your seats again.''

He raised his eyebrows when they immediately obeyed and hurried back to their desks. Wow. The woman knew how to run a tight ship. Who would have thought someone as meek as she seemed to be could command instant order with her students?

"Can we help you with something, Chief Harte?''

He was pretty sure that tight schoolmarm voice shouldn't turn him on so much, especially with a classroom full of interested fourth graders looking on. It shouldn't be able to slide through his bones, settle in his gut.

He was a bad, bad boy and the idea of pulling her silky hair from its clip, undoing that sweater a button or two and seeing if he could make even more color soak that honey-soft skin appealed to him far more than it should.

He was sick.

He had to be, to entertain prurient fantasies about a sweet, shy schoolteacher like Sarah McKenzie.

He reined in his rampaging thoughts, shifted his weight and turned his attention to the class. He recognized most of the students from around town. Near the back he found Corey Sylvester, sitting alone and looking very aloof. The boy met his gaze warily, then looked down at the book open on his desk.

Was he acting guilty or just resigned to what he had already figured out was coming?

Jesse couldn't tell. How would the kid react if he singled him out in front of his whole class? If he yanked him out into the hall and started grilling him like a suspect? It sure as hell wouldn't put the kid in any kind of mood to chat about who or what was causing his mysterious accidents.

Chuck Hendricks and his suspicious little mind could go to the devil, he decided abruptly. He would run this investigation his own way.

He turned back to Sarah with a smile. To his guilty amusement, the color dusting her cheeks turned a darker shade. "I'm sorry to interrupt, Miss McKenzie. Could I take a few moments of your class time?"

"I...of course."

"Thanks. I'll make it brief and then you can get back to whatever you were doing."

"Math," his new niece, Dylan, said with a disgusted sigh. The implication in her voice was obvious: *Take as long as you want. We don't mind.* He swallowed a sympathetic grin and turned to the rest of the class.

"I suppose you've all heard by now that somebody broke in to the school last night and took the money you've been collecting for the hospital."

As he expected, the students buzzed with reaction, from boos and hisses to shocked exclamations by those who hadn't heard. He registered them all, but kept his gaze on Corey. Unless he was mistaken, Corey looked as upset as the rest of the class.

A redheaded boy covered in freckles—Paul Turner's kid, if Jesse wasn't mistaken—raised his hand. "You catch who did it yet, Chief?"

"Not yet. But I'm going to, I promise you that. I'll need your help, though."

Jackie Allsop, who had won the Little Buckeroo mutton-bustin' competition at the county fair two years running, raised her hand. "Are you puttin' a posse together?"

He swallowed another grin. "Something like that.

See, the way I figure it, it's not right that somebody can come in and take something that you all and your friends have worked so hard to earn. Money you intended to be used to help sick kids. It's not fair. It makes me mad and it should make you mad, too.''

Their outraged reaction filled the room. Out of the corner of his gaze, he saw Sarah frown. Uh-oh. Before she could step forward to quiet her students, he held up his hands. The students immediately quieted. ''I appreciate your spirit. That's what it's going to take to catch whoever did this because, to be honest with you, we don't have a lot to go on right now.''

''How can we help, Uncle Jess?'' Lucy asked in her soft voice.

He smiled at her. ''Good question, Luce. I want all of you to use your eyes and your ears for me. You have to promise me you won't do anything dangerous, though. If you hear anything you think might help us find whoever took the money, you need to let a grown-up know, okay? Either tell your mom and dad or Miss McKenzie or me. What are some of the things you could be on the lookout for?''

For the next few moments all the children—even the quiet ones—vied with each other to give suggestions, and Sarah watched their enthusiasm with amazement. Jesse had quite a way with children. She should have expected it by the adoration Lucy, and now Dylan, had for him, but she was still surprised at the way her students hung on his every word.

He managed to stir up participation from the entire class as if he had been teaching all his life.

She was going to have a tough time trying to get them to focus on fractions after this kind of excitement, she thought with a sigh. Who was she kidding? Forget the kids. She would be lucky to get through math herself today.

"Thanks for all your great ideas." To her relief, Jesse started to wrap things up. "Now I have to get back to work trying to find out who did it. Remember, if you hear or see something that might help solve the case, who are you going to tell?"

"A grown-up!" the class chorused.

He turned the full power of his smile on them. Even though she was just out of range of it, Sarah still felt the impact of that smile sizzle clear down to her toes. Darn it. The man had no business coming into her classroom and sabotaging her concentration like this.

To her dismay, when he finished addressing the class he headed toward her. "Can I talk to you out in the hall for a minute?" he asked, his voice low enough to send shivers rippling down her spine.

Out in the hall? Just the two of them? When she felt as rattled as seed pods in a strong breeze?

She could handle it, she reminded herself. She was turning over a new leaf and putting all her anxieties behind her. Right? A few minutes alone in the hall with Jesse Harte would be fine. Completely fine.

"Of course," she answered coolly. "Students, turn your attention to today's math assignment. If you have any questions about the work sheet, I'll be back in a few moments to answer them."

Ignoring their grumbles, she set her teacher's guide on her desk, then led the way out into the hall.

Jesse followed her with the strangest look on his face. If she didn't know better, she might have thought it was masculine interest, but of course it couldn't be.

He seemed extremely fascinated by her hair, though. She spent a brief, horrible moment wondering if she'd smeared paint in it while she was preparing the art supplies for the day. She almost reached a hand to check, then let it fall to her side, feeling extremely foolish.

"My students are waiting, Chief Harte," she finally said. "How may I help you?"

"Jess. Call me Jess. Everybody does."

Yes, she knew. Jesse James Harte, the outlaw cop. "If this is about the stolen money, Chief Harte—er, Jess—I'm afraid I can't help you. I don't know anything."

"It's more about one of your students. I need to ask your advice."

She stiffened. "Do you suspect one of my students was involved?"

"Up-Chuck is convinced Corey stole the money."

"Up-Chuck?" she asked, momentarily diverted.

"Er, Principal Hendricks. Sorry. You know what they say about old habits. It's been a long time since sixth grade, but it's still tough for me to think of him as anything else."

She could just imagine him in sixth grade, cocky and tough and rebellious.

A teacher's worst nightmare.

And a sixth-grade girl's biggest fantasy.

She jerked her mind away from that dangerous road. "What possible reason does he have to accuse Corey, besides the fact that he blames the poor boy for every single thing that goes wrong in this entire school?"

"He says he's seen Corey hanging around the jar several times in the last week, looking at the coins inside."

She bristled. "Since when does looking at something make you a criminal? If that's the case, arrest me now.

Sometimes I like to walk through the art galleries in Jackson and dream about owning some of the works hanging there. That must make me some kind of international art thief, right?''

"Which ones?"

"Which ones what?"

"Which art galleries do you like?"

"What difference does it make?" she asked impatiently. "My point is, I can't believe you would base your entire investigation on the suspicions of a nasty, small-minded little man."

"I didn't say I agreed with him," Jesse protested. "I'm just telling you his theory."

"So that's why you're really here? To interrogate a child?"

She knew she sounded judgmental, shrewish even, but she didn't care. All her hard work trying to gain Corey's trust these past few weeks would be for nothing if she handed him over to Chief Harte like a trussed goose for Christmas dinner.

"I'd like to talk to him, not interrogate him. I would have pulled him out of class, but I figured the rest of your students didn't need to speculate about why the two of us might need to have a little chat."

She narrowed her gaze at him, studying him closely. She didn't know him nearly well enough to know whether he was telling the truth, but she would have to trust her instincts. All she could see gleaming out of his deep blue eyes was sincerity.

"That was very thoughtful of you," she murmured. "Corey has a hard enough time getting along with his classmates. To be marked as a thief would make him a pariah. I'm afraid children don't readily understand the concept of innocent until proven guilty."

"Neither do certain principals I could name."

She smiled. "Right."

He returned her smile with a grin that made him seem much more like that mischievous sixth grader he'd referred to earlier. Her pulse fluttered wildly and she finally dropped her gaze to her hands. "I really do need to get back to my class. Is there anything else I can help you with?"

"Yeah. I'm still going to have to talk to Corey so I can clear him as a suspect and get on with the investigation. I just wanted some advice on the best tack to take with him. You seem to have a rapport with him."

"I don't know about that." She thought about the boy's surliness since he had come into her class. He had begun to unbend a little, but she knew she still had a long way to go before earning his trust.

"Is there some time during the day I could talk to him without the rest of the class around?" Jesse asked.

She thought a moment. "Yes, actually, there is. Around twelve-thirty, during lunch recess. You could talk to him then. He has to stay in because he didn't turn in his homework folder last week. It's, um, one of our classroom rules." Why did she suddenly feel so defensive, as if she were the strictest teacher in the school?

Jesse didn't seem to notice. "Sounds like a plan. And I'll bring you lunch so I have an excuse for being here. That way he'll think I'm only here to see you."

She wasn't at all sure she wanted her students to think she and Chief Harte had something going. They didn't. Of course they didn't. Two people couldn't possibly be more mismatched—he caught criminals for a living and she was afraid of her own shadow.

"Murphy's got a special on fettuccine Alfredo this week," Jesse went on. "How does that sound?"

"Lunch is really not necessary, Chief Harte. I'm sure you can come up with another excuse for dropping in to the classroom."

"It's the least I can do for your help." He gave her another one of those devastating smiles, the ones that made her feel as if her legs had no more substance to them than Mr. Murphy's fettuccine.

Arguing with him would make her sound even more like an idiot. Besides, she had a sneaking suspicion Jesse Harte was fairly used to getting his own way.

Lunch wouldn't hurt her. Hadn't she just been thinking how tired she was of eating alone? Here was her chance for a little conversation.

But as she watched him walk away down the hall with that purposeful stride, she had the sudden, terrifying certainty that she had just agreed to dine with the devil.

Chapter 6

He couldn't remember when he'd ever looked forward so eagerly to taking a statement. But then again, few of his interviews had the fringe benefit of including lunch with a sweet, pretty schoolteacher who blushed like a rose in full bloom.

Whistling in anticipation, Jesse reached into the back seat of his vehicle and grabbed the bag of takeout he had just picked up from the diner. As a rule, Murphy didn't normally fix takeout, but Jesse had had no qualms about cashing in some favors the café owner owed him. He now had two servings of Murphy's world-famous fettuccine Alfredo and all the trimmings in his possession.

He just hoped he could convince Sarah to eat it with him.

He wanted to talk to Corey about the missing money, but he also wanted to get to the bottom of the mystery that was Sarah McKenzie. This seemed like a golden opportunity to do it.

For the second time that day he walked through the front doors of Salt River Elementary. Through the glass walls of the office he could see Chuck wagging his finger at some hapless student slumped in one of the hard plastic chairs.

The principal spied Jesse as soon as he walked inside. Chuck froze in midwag, then changed the gesture to a crooked-finger demand for Jesse to come into his office. Pretending he didn't notice, he continued down the hall toward Sarah's room. Let Up-Chuck come find *him* if he was itching to have a chat so badly.

The school was much more quiet now than it had been earlier in the morning, probably because all the kids were either at lunch or out on the playground for recess.

At Sarah's classroom he peeked around the corner, through the open doorway. She was the only one in the room, bent over her desk with a black gradebook in front of her and her hair a shimmering gold curtain flowing down her back.

That sinfully gorgeous hair ought to be against the law. It seemed such an erotic contrast with both the innocent schoolroom setting and her frown of concentration that he had to swallow hard.

A few seconds later she sensed his presence. She looked up and he thought he saw just a quick flash of jittery awareness before she blinked it away and gave him a polite smile instead. Too bad. He preferred jittery awareness any day.

He held up the bag from the café. ''I brought lunch. Murphy makes a killer Alfredo sauce. Do we have time to eat before Corey comes in for detention?''

She frowned. "Fifteen minutes or so. But I thought I told you not to bother with lunch."

"Hmm. And I thought I told you I wanted to bother. Come on, Sarah. Humor me."

She sighed but didn't argue, which he took as a relatively positive sign. He held the bag up again. "Murphy put together the works for us. Salad, bread sticks and pie for dessert. Where do you want it?"

With another sigh, she scanned the classroom. "That worktable back by the computers is empty. We can sit there."

The next few moments were spent pulling up chairs and setting out containers. Murphy was a saint. He had even included paper plates and plastic dinnerware, something Jesse hadn't even thought about.

The one thing neither he nor Murphy had covered was a beverage, but Sarah solved the problem by going to a minirefrigerator behind her desk and pulling out two bottles of water.

He piled food on a plate for her, then did the same for himself, all the while aware of her sitting across the table watching him with the same wariness in her big eyes that he'd seen in Corey Sylvester's.

The food was divine, just as he expected. The sauce was rich and creamy, the bread sticks just crispy enough and the salad was fresh and tasted like springtime.

Sarah didn't eat enough to keep a kitten alive, though. Maybe that was the reason the bones at her wrists seemed so fragile.

"Do you always push your food around your plate," he finally asked, "or is it the company?"

She looked up, startled. "I'm sorry," she said. "The food is wonderful. Delicious. And it was very thought-

ful of you to bring it. I guess I'm not very hungry right
now.''

Maybe she was just painfully shy. Maybe he was
torturing her by continuing to force himself on her
when she was obviously so nervous around him. The
kindest thing would probably be to quit pestering her,
to just stay out of her way.

He wasn't at all sure why the idea was so repugnant
to him. And anyway, the few times he'd seen her with
other people she'd been friendly and composed. He
was the only one who seemed to make her edgy and
uptight, and damned if he didn't want to know why—
and what had put those shadows in her eyes.

Besides, he hadn't been kind in a long, long time.

''So tell me about Chicago,'' he asked abruptly.

She nearly knocked over her water bottle.
''Wh…what?''

''Chicago. What was it like teaching there?''

She was silent for a several moments and he thought
she was going to ignore the question, then she smiled
softly. ''It was great. Really great. I loved my students.
It was an incredible feeling to know I could make such
a difference in their lives.''

''You taught elementary school?''

''Yes. Third grade, a year younger than my students
here. It was a fairly rough neighborhood and some of
my students lived in the most hideous conditions you
can imagine. Without heat or running water, even. And
I suspect that for many of them, school lunch was the
only square meal they had all day. But despite their
hardships, they all had so much promise. They were
starving for far more than food. They needed someone
to show them what they could achieve in life.''

''And you tried to do that?''

"As best I could. Sometimes it was tough, I won't deny that, but I loved the challenge. I found that with a little creativity, I could usually find something that interested them—sports or animals or music or whatever—and individualize each student's curriculum around his or her interests. It really worked."

When the subject was teaching, she glowed with enthusiasm, with bright energy, and he couldn't take his gaze off her. She was like some rare, precious flower that bloomed only under exactly the right conditions. Now that he'd seen her vivid petals unfurl, he knew he wouldn't be content with just this one fleeting glimpse.

"Why didn't you stay?" he asked.

Wrong question. He regretted it instantly when her animation died just like a frost-killed blossom. That haunted look flashed across her eyes again before she quickly shuttered them.

"Every job has its good and bad points." Her voice was stiff and bleak.

"True enough. My job is usually great, but every once in a while I have to deal with the Chuck Hendrickses of the world."

Her expression thawed a little. "What are you complaining about? I have to deal with him every day."

He smiled even as he fought the wholly inappropriate urge to press his lips to the corner of that mouth that lifted so endearingly.

As if she could tell exactly what he was thinking, her breathing quickened and she became fascinated with the pasta she twirled around and around her fork. "What about you? Have you always wanted to work in law enforcement?"

His own smile slid away as he thought of those days and months and years when the only thing he wanted was another drink to dull the guilt. He doubted a woman like Sarah McKenzie would know anything about a world so sordid and dark.

"Would it shock you if I told you I decided to become a cop one night when I was in jail?"

Her gaze flew to his, then she colored again. "How am I supposed to answer that? No matter what I say, I sound like a prissy schoolteacher. You're making that up, right?"

He laughed, but it held little humor. "It's true. I was twenty-one years old and in the joint again for a D and D—drunk and disorderly. This time I'd made the mistake of planting a right hook on the officer who came to break up the bar fight I was relishing at the time of my arrest, so old Chief Briggs added assaulting a police officer to my charges."

He sipped at his water bottle. "Unfortunately, I didn't have enough cash on me to pay the necessary bribe and persuade Salt River's finest to look the other way. That's the way things worked in those days."

"That's terrible!"

"Carl Briggs, the previous police chief, ran his own little fiefdom. He was a real prize. Anyway, I realized that arrest would stick on my record and there wasn't a thing I could do about it."

"And that was a turning point for you?"

He nodded. "I can remember lying on that scratchy wool blanket in my cell and looking out the little window at the night. I was hungover and battered and bleeding from the bit of extra attention I received from a couple of nightsticks. I felt like an old man. In that moment, I decided I was tired of being on the wrong side of the law. At the rate I was going, I was going to end up dead or doing some hard time in the state pen, so I decided right then that things would change.''

He gave her a wicked smile. ''I was a bad boy when I was younger, Ms. McKenzie. The kind your mama probably warned you about.''

She raised her eyebrows. ''Since we've already established that I sound like a prissy schoolteacher, I must ask. Just how, exactly, have you changed since then?''

Damned if she didn't make him feel fourteen years old still lighting bottle rockets in the mayor's mailbox. He laughed. ''You're probably right. I'm still a hell-raiser. I just try to do it on the right side of the law this time.''

Once more that flicker of awareness flashed across her green eyes like distant lightning on a July night. His gaze landed on her mouth, tracing the curve of her lips.

As he watched, her pink tongue darted out to lick that little indentation in the center of her top lip where mouth met skin. It was a completely guileless gesture, probably a nervous reaction to him staring at her mouth, but it reached right into his gut and gave a hard tug.

His pulse seemed suddenly thick and heavy through his veins. Like a slow trickling creek in the middle of August.

He wanted to be the one licking at her lips. Gliding over that lush, soft mouth, tasting whatever memory of butter and cream remained from Murphy's killer Alfredo sauce.

No. He couldn't.

But his body was already angling toward her, his head already leaning to hers. Her eyes widened with alarm—or was it anticipation?—then her lips parted slightly.

He took that as assent. What the hell else could he do? He would die if he didn't kiss her. His mouth was almost to hers when the sound of her classroom door opening echoed in the room like a gunshot.

Sarah froze, exhaling a puff of air that skimmed over his lips as erotically as their might-have-been kiss, then she jerked away from him as if he'd yanked her hair.

She turned toward the door, fierce color spreading over her cheeks in a hot, angry tide. "Corey! Come in."

The boy sauntered into the classroom, his usual air of defiance and belligerence firmly in place. Sarah didn't seem to notice. "Uh, thank you for coming so quickly," she said distractedly. "Did you have time to finish your lunch?"

Corey shrugged. "Much as I could stand."

"Was it awful?"

"Chipped beef on toast. Yuck. Least they had apple crumble for dessert."

"Good for you to come up with a bright side to chipped beef on toast!" She smiled at Corey and Jesse realized with mild shock that she genuinely cared about the kid, despite the troublemaker attitude he wore as proudly as Jesse wore his badge. It was obvious from her smile and her body language and the affection in her eyes. What's more, Corey knew it was real, and he obviously adored her for it.

Jesse remembered her passionate defense of the boy against Chuck's suspicions earlier in the day and her willingness to go to the authorities with her fear about Corey's home life.

To his chagrin, he experienced a flash of sudden and

completely unreasonable jealousy. It wasn't only the grim knowledge that she would probably never look at him with that same affection. He suddenly realized he couldn't remember any of his teachers ever looking at him like that, ever being willing to stand up for him or take his side of things. If they had, he probably would have liked school a whole lot more.

So what made Sarah different than the other teachers Corey had gone through?

Maybe she had a soft spot in her heart for bad boys.

"What's the chief doin' here?" Corey asked.

Jesse answered before Sarah could. "Having lunch with Ms. McKenzie. We're friends." At least, he thought he wanted them to be.

Corey took in the scattered plates and takeout containers on the table, then looked back at the two of them. His sharp little face twisted into a frown. "Yeah? I didn't know stupid cops had any friends."

Now, where did that sudden animosity come from? "Some of us even get married and have families, amazingly enough," Jesse answered.

Corey looked completely aghast at the idea. As his gaze darted between the two of them, Jesse realized something else enlightening. The tough kid of Salt River Elementary had a crush on his pretty blond teacher.

Sarah seemed oblivious to it. "If you're still hungry, I have some pasta left. You're more than welcome to eat it, Corey."

"Looks like chipped beef on noodles," he muttered.

"It's much better," she assured him, but the boy didn't look convinced. "How about some pie, then?"

This was obviously much more appealing to Corey.

He grabbed for a piece with a mumbled thanks and dug right in to it.

"I have to finish recording a few grades," Sarah said after a moment. "When you're done with your pie, why don't you wash your hands and clean out Raticus's cage? I'm sure Chief Harte would love to give you a hand with our class pet."

"Oh, yes. Love to," he said dryly. A pet rat. Great. Still, it was a chance for a little private time to talk to Corey and he couldn't pass up the opportunity, even if it entailed cleaning out a rodent's cage.

His job apparently was to hold the rat while Corey put new paper in the bottom of his cage and refilled the water and food dishes. Jesse held the animal gingerly.

In his year spent at the police academy, he had never expected to end up in a fourth-grade classroom holding a rat.

He held Raticus up closer. The rat watched him out of beady little eyes, his whiskers and pink tail twitching. "Does this charming little rodent bite?" Jesse asked.

Corey snorted. "Only if you bite him first."

"I think it's safe to say that's not going to happen anytime soon."

The boy's amusement was fleeting. He quickly returned to glowering. "Don't you have crime to fight or somethin'?"

"I'm on my lunch hour."

"I thought you said you wouldn't rest until you found whoever stole the school money."

The rat wiggled around in his hands and Jesse had to tighten his grip. "I'll find him. Don't worry about it."

"Who said I was worried? I don't care about any stupid quarter jar for any stupid hospital."

"You put any quarters in that stupid jar?"

Corey refused to meet his gaze as he poured food into a small dish. "So what if I did? It was my own money. My mom gave it to me so I could get a pop on my way home from school."

Damn Chuck Hendricks and his suspicious little mind. The only reason Corey had been hanging around the quarter jar was to covertly drop some coins in.

Chuck couldn't even give the kid credit for good intentions when the evidence was right in front of his face. He had to attribute ulterior motives to everything.

The kid had sacrificed his own wants and needs to help sick children the only way he knew how.

Jesse's chest felt suddenly tight. He wanted to give the kid's shoulder a squeeze, to tell him he was proud of him for caring, but he checked the impulse—not just because his hands were full of rat, but because he'd been that cocky kid once upon a time, afraid to show any emotion.

Corey wouldn't welcome the gesture, wouldn't know how to deal with it, any more than Jesse would have at that age.

He cleared his throat. "As I said to the class before, it burns me that somebody took that money that you and the rest of the kids worked so hard for. You haven't heard anything about who might have taken it, have you?"

"Why would you think I know anything?"

Jesse weighed his words. "A street-smart kid like you keeps his ear to the ground. You probably know more about what goes on in this town than I do."

Corey snorted. "That's not too tough."

"If you hear anything, you'll let me know, right?"

"Whatever." The boy reached for the rat to return him to his clean cage and Jesse handed it over willingly.

The two of them watched Raticus settle in for a moment, then walked together back to Sarah's desk.

"All done?" she asked.

"Yeah," Corey said.

"Thank you. Lunch recess is almost over. Why don't you work in your handwriting notebook until the other children return?"

He made a face but returned to his desk, leaving Jesse and Sarah alone at her desk.

He gestured toward the hall, where they could talk without the boy overhearing. "Did you learn anything?" she asked when they were out of range.

"He wouldn't have taken the money. Not after he sacrificed his own after-school treat so he could put some change in the jar."

"I knew it." Satisfaction glinted in her green eyes. "Now what?"

"I get the pleasure of telling Chuck he's crazy." He grinned.

She smiled back and his gaze froze on her mouth, the memory of their almost-kiss surging through his veins like the whiskey he didn't drink anymore.

He could do it. Right now. Could dip his head and taste her, right here in the middle of the elementary school hallway.

He almost did. He was just a hairbreadth away from dipping his head to hers and taking that sweet mouth. At the last minute, reality returned with stunning force.

"I've got to run," he said abruptly, stepping back. "Thanks for lunch."

"I…you're welcome."

What was he doing? he asked himself as he walked out of the building. He had no business trying to steal a kiss from her—not once, but twice. No business imagining that incredible golden hair sliding through his fingers, no business wondering about that slender body underneath her demure clothes.

She had wanted him to kiss her, both times. He had seen it in the softening of her mouth, in the wary attraction sparkling in her eyes like Christmas lights.

But he wouldn't. She was too sweetly innocent for a man like him. Too fragile. If he kissed her, she wouldn't have the first idea how to handle it.

Sarah McKenzie wasn't his type. He would hurt her. He might not mean to, but he would. That's just the kind of woman she was.

If he were smart, he would put all his energy into keeping those kinds of inappropriate thoughts about her right out of his head.

She simply had to stop thinking about Jesse Harte.

Hours later, alone in her silent little house with the curtains drawn tightly against the dark, rainy night, Sarah couldn't keep her mind off the man, off those brief moments in her classroom and later in the hallway when she thought—feared? hoped?—he would kiss her.

It had taken hours to even make a dent in reading the weekly assignments for Writer's Workshop. She tried hard to concentrate. But every few pages she would find herself back in that classroom, inhaling the masculine, woodsy scent of his aftershave, watching the muscle in his jaw twitch, trying fiercely to remember to breathe when that mouth started to lower to hers.

What would she have done if he'd kissed her? Would she have panicked? Found herself back in the throes of a flashback she couldn't control? Or would she have welcomed it, reveled in it?

She had wanted desperately to find out. She still did, if she were honest with herself.

She sighed. Might as well wish for the moon while she was at it. A man like Jesse Harte wouldn't possibly be interested in a woman like her.

He was the most eligible bachelor in Salt River. Every woman in town probably swooned over him. He radiated strength and power. Vitality.

Was that why she was so attracted to him? Because he seemed to represent everything she was not? She was a timid, prissy schoolteacher afraid of even Raticus. It was no wonder Jesse hadn't followed through on the look in his eyes and kissed her.

She set her red pencil down, depressed all over again. She ought to just go to sleep—it was past midnight, after all, and she was far from being productive.

The idea of facing that solitary bed, with those cold, lonely sheets and an empty pillow and nightmares lurking in the corners was about as appealing as sleeping out in the rain. But she had to recharge her batteries somehow if she had any hope of coping with thirty unruly ten-year-olds the next day.

She began her nightly ritual, checking and double-checking the locks on the windows and doors. At the back door she paused, looking out the small window at the drizzly night and the little backyard she was slowly transforming into a garden.

A cat yowled somewhere, a dog barked sharply in answer, and the wet breeze fluttered the silvery wind chimes she'd bought the week before in Jackson. She smiled a little at the small-town quiet she had come to love and was just ready to head to her room when a blur of movement outside the glow of the porch lights caught her attention.

She stiffened as her eyes adjusted to the dark, as the blur became a more solid shape.

Cold fear turned her blood to ice.

Someone was out there!

Chapter 7

"Would you like another cookie, dear?"

Jesse ground his back teeth. At this rate he'd be here all night. "No, thank you, Mrs. Lehman. It's late. Why don't we just get to your report?"

"Are you sure? I know they're your favorites."

One of the hazards of working his whole life in the same small town where he grew up was that everybody thought they knew every single thing about him. For one terrible summer when he was nine, Doris Lehman had attempted to give him piano lessons. They had both barely survived the ordeal.

At least she didn't appear to hold a grudge.

"Thanks, anyway, but I'm full." Jesse fought back a yawn and tried to stay focused. Working three double watches in a row would kill him if Mrs. Lehman's butter-rich shortbread cookies didn't do the job first.

Ignoring him, she hoisted her tiny frame out of her chair using her carved, ivory-handled cane and creaked toward the kitchen, her yippy little poodle dancing around her feet. It was past midnight, but the elderly woman was still fully dressed and looked as elegant as if she were on her way to the opera.

"I'll just put a few cookies in a bag, dear, and you can take them with you for later."

With a resigned sigh, Jesse followed her and the poodle into her kitchen. Mrs. Lehman was in the mood to chat. She did this every few weeks or so, called him or his officers to her house on some trumped-up disturbance call. Most of the time he didn't mind. She'd been lonely since her husband, Ed, had died three years earlier and he had instructed his officers to visit with her for a while, no matter how outlandish the complaint, just to make sure she was okay.

He sighed again. It wasn't always easy to follow your own advice.

"That's very nice of you, Mrs. Lehman," he said. "Now, about what you thought you saw tonight…?"

She shook her cane at him, damn near poking his eye out. "Don't use that tone of voice with me, young man, like you're just humoring a crazy old bat by even being here. I saw what I saw. No question about that."

"Can we go over exactly what you saw, then?"

"Not if you're going to patronize me."

He huffed out a breath. He was too blasted tired for this tonight. "What did you see, Mrs. Lehman?" he asked patiently.

She squinted at him for a moment, then finally spoke, apparently satisfied that his interest was genuine. "Lights, up on Elk Mountain. This is the third night in a row I've seen them. They don't belong there."

"Maybe it's high schoolers out four-wheeling or somebody spotlighting for deer."

"I don't think so. These lights didn't move at all. And they didn't look normal, either, I'll tell you that."

"What do you mean?"

"Just what I said." She shifted her gaze around the room as if she feared eavesdroppers, then she lowered her voice. "I think I might know what they're from."

"What?" He leaned forward, pitching his own voice low.

"Aliens."

He leaned back, blinking hard. Maybe Mrs. Lehman needed to have her medication levels checked. "Aliens?"

"Right."

"What gives you that idea?"

"I know all about government conspiracies, young man. About Roswell and Area 54 and black helicopters. I watch *The X-Files,* you know."

"And you think Salt River is in the middle of some kind of alien invasion?"

"I think you need to drive up there to Elk Mountain and check it out. But you'll have to be careful. Don't go alone, whatever you do. Who knows what would happen if they caught you?"

"I shudder to think," he said, hiding his amusement. Mrs. Lehman might have some crazy ideas, but she was usually harmless. "Thanks for calling this to our attention. Technically, Elk Mountain would be the county's jurisdiction, though. Lucky for me, any alien problem would be Sheriff Mitchell's responsibility."

"What are you going to do?"

"Why don't you give me a call the next time you see the lights so I can look up there too and pinpoint exactly where they're coming from and I'll check it out. Okay?''

Before she could answer, the radio at his waist crackled. He pressed the button. ''Yeah. Harte here.''

His evening dispatcher's voice crackled through the static. ''Chief, I have a report of an attempted break-in. Four-oh-four Spruce Street.''

His pulse lurched. That was Sarah's address!

''Maybe it's the aliens!'' Mrs. Lehman exclaimed, her brown eyes bright with horrified excitement. ''Maybe they're looking for some poor soul to use for their experiments.''

He was already heading for the door. ''I certainly hope not. Look, Mrs. Lehman, I'm the only officer on duty tonight. Can you give your report tomorrow at the station?''

''Why, certainly, dear. You'd better hurry. Here. Don't forget your cookies.''

He drove the three blocks to Spruce Street in record time. Every light in Sarah's little gingerbread house was blazing when he pulled up. He shut off the engine and raced to the door, then pounded hard.

''Sarah? It's Jess. Open up.''

It took a painfully long time for her to come to the door, while a hundred grim scenarios flashed through his brain. Finally, just before he would have knocked the damn thing down, the lace curtain in the small window fluttered, then her face peered out, her features wary.

Her eyes widened with recognition—and a vast, glimmering relief, he thought—then he heard the snick of a lock. A moment later, she opened the door to him.

''Chief Harte. Thank you for responding so quickly,'' she murmured.

He might have expected her to be hysterical, judging by her panicked reaction to him the other day. Her face was pale, but otherwise she seemed calm. On closer inspection, he could see that her hands trembled slightly, like a child who has been too long out in the cold.

She wore a robe patterned in rich jewel tones, which only seemed to make her skin look more fragile, a ghostly, bloodless white.

The sudden, powerful urge to gather her up, tuck her against his chest and keep her safe and warm there forever erupted out of nowhere, scaring the hell out of him.

Knowing it was completely inappropriate—not to mention that it would probably terrify her senseless—he struggled into his concerned-but-dispassionate-cop routine. "I had a report of a possible break-in at this address."

The emerald lapels of her silky robe rose and fell when she breathed deeply, as if fighting for control. "I...yes. That's right."

"Are you all right?"

"Yes. Fine." She fidgeted with the sash on her robe. "I just feel so silly. I shouldn't have bothered you."

"Of course you should bother us. That's why we're here."

"I'm not even sure I saw anything now. It was so dark."

"Why don't we sit down and you can tell me exactly what you thought you saw?"

After a moment's hesitation, she chose a rose-colored wingback chair near the cold fireplace and perched on the edge, hands clasped tightly together in her lap. He took the couch and stretched his long legs out, then pulled his notebook from his breast pocket.

"How long ago did you see the intruder?"

Her hands fluttered. "I told you, I'm not even sure it was someone trying to break in."

"That's what I'm here to figure out, sweetheart. How long ago?"

"Fifteen minutes, maybe."

"And what happened?"

She closed her eyes as if trying to re-create the events in her mind. "I was grading papers at the kitchen table and couldn't concentrate."

Her gaze met his suddenly, then two bright spots of color appeared high on her cheekbones, making him wonder what, exactly, had destroyed her concentration.

She quickly jerked her gaze away. "I decided to go to bed. I was just turning off the lights and checking the locks. I thought I saw something move. I figured it was a cat or something, but then I…I saw a man standing there."

"Standing where?"

"Off the back porch." She frowned, wrinkles of concentration creasing her forehead. "Actually, just at the bottom of the steps."

"Did you get a look at him?"

"No. He was just outside the porch lights, and it was so dark. I just saw a shape, really."

"Did he appear large or small? Was he as tall as me?"

Her gaze flashed to him again, then she gazed down at her hands. "He seemed huge," she said, her voice small and tight. "But I don't really know. I was so frightened I couldn't think straight."

"I'll just put a question mark here on size, then."

"I'm probably imagining the whole thing. I'm so sorry I dragged you out here."

He thought of old Mrs. Lehman and her alien visitors. Sarah McKenzie seeing a dark stranger lurking on her back step didn't even compare. "Let me take a look around," he said. "If you think someone was trying to break in, I believe you."

At his words, her face softened and her eyes went dewy and huge as if she was going to cry. "Thank you," she said softly. "I'm still going to feel ridiculous when you don't find anything."

"Don't worry about it. Just relax, have a cup of tea or something, and I'll be back in a few moments."

She nodded. "Be careful, okay?"

Her concern for his safety climbed right in and settled in his heart. Just how was he supposed to keep a safe emotional distance between them when she said something like that, something that made this odd warmth steal through him?

He couldn't remember the last time somebody had worried about him. His family loved him, he knew that, but they had realized a long time ago that he could take care of himself.

Not at all sure whether he liked the feeling, he left Sarah sitting by her empty fireplace and walked out into the soggy night.

A cool drizzle settled in his hair and beaded on the oiled canvas of his coat. He barely noticed, narrowing his focus only on the job as he scoured the scene for any sign that someone had indeed been trying to break in to Sarah's house.

The gleam from his flashlight turned up little. All looked normal on her cozy little back porch—no overturned planters or dislodged cushions that he could tell.

Her backyard was fenced only on three sides. Anyone could sneak from the road around to the rear of the house. If someone wanted to break in, it made sense that he would go around to the back, where criminal activities wouldn't be as noticeable from the street.

He walked down the steps and down a small gravel pathway that curved around the house. There. There was something. He crouched, shining the beam of his flashlight into the flower garden between the walkway and the house. The light gleamed off the print of what looked like a man's work boot in the mud, as if someone had misstepped off the pathway.

It wasn't much to go on. It hadn't rained hard that day, so for all he knew, it could have been left earlier by a meter reader or Bob Jimenez, her landlord. But it was all he could see in the dark.

A careful look around the small house revealed little else, other than the interesting tidbit that Sarah Mc-Kenzie appeared to be an avid gardener, judging by all the upturned earth around the house.

She must spend every spare second she wasn't teaching outside with her hands in the dirt. The thought of the quiet, skittish schoolteacher pouring her heart and soul into creating beauty around her touched him in ways he couldn't explain.

He didn't know too many renters who would put such care and effort into beautifying a house they didn't own. Hell, he could barely manage to keep the grass mowed in the summertime around the place he'd bought after he made chief.

But Sarah was a nurturer. Plants, children, whatever. Would she go for neat, ordered gardens, he wondered, where no flower would dare touch the next and all were arranged in some precise pattern according to shade, color or height?

Or would she prefer wild jumbles of color? Frenzied splotches of yellows and reds and purples growing every which way?

It seemed logical to assume a quiet schoolteacher would prefer a prim and proper garden. But some instinct told him that in a month or so the yard around her house would burst with lush, unrestrained beauty.

He had a feeling that for all her subdued reticence, there were hidden depths to Sarah that fairly begged to be discovered.

But not by him. He'd leave any exploring of Sarah McKenzie's deeper passions to some other man.

Some better man.

A guy who could give her happily-ever-after, a white picket fence and all the flowers and children she could ask for.

Why should that thought depress him so much?

It was none of his business. *She* was none of his business, other than one of the citizens of Salt River he was sworn to protect.

Keeping that firmly in mind, he forced his attention back to the investigation and finished walking the perimeter of her house. When he finished, he rapped hard on her door. She opened immediately, almost as if she'd been standing just inside watching and waiting for him.

She could tell instantly by the regretful look in his eyes that he hadn't found anything substantial.

Had she imagined the whole thing? Had she been having another of those damn flashbacks again and somehow merged nightmare with reality?

She must have been. What other explanation could there be? She had been seeing things.

Anger at herself and an awful, painful embarrassment warred within her. After this and the way she'd freaked out the other day on her back porch, he probably thought she was the most ridiculous, paranoid schoolmarm who ever lived.

She had a fierce, painfully futile wish that Jesse Harte could have known her Before.

When she had been fun and adventurous and whole. When she drew people to her just like an ice-cream shop does on a warm summer day.

When she never saw strangers lurking in the shadows or panicked if a man touched her or had bouts where she stood in the shower for hours, scrubbing and scrubbing but somehow never coming clean.

"You didn't find anything," she said, a statement not a question.

"A bootprint in the mud. Other than that, nothing."

"I'm sorry." She clasped her hands together tightly, wishing she'd never called the police, wishing a different officer had responded, wishing she could sink right through the carpet and disappear. "You must think I'm the most foolish woman in town."

He grinned suddenly, looking impossibly gorgeous. "Not even close, sweetheart. You're not calling me to report seeing little green men in spaceships."

"No. Only bogeymen who don't exist."

"Sarah, if you think you saw a man out there, I believe you. Just because I can't see anything to prove it beyond a shadow of a doubt doesn't mean the guy wasn't there. It might have been a kid looking to steal some tools or just a peeping Tom hoping to get lucky and find an open curtain somewhere."

She couldn't help her instinctive shudder at the idea of someone watching her without her knowledge.

Jesse's cop eyes picked up on her reaction. "It's probably nothing for you to worry about," he assured her. "I'll cruise around the neighborhood and see if I can find any suspicious characters lurking around and I'll also put an extra patrol in this neighborhood for a while."

"Thank you. I... You've been very kind."

He gave her an inscrutable look. "Call me immediately if you see anything else suspicious. Try to get some sleep, okay?"

She nodded, then watched him walk back out into the drizzly night. A week ago, she never would have even considered the word *kind* in the same sentence as Jesse Harte. He was hard and dangerous and he scared the stuffing out of her. But something had changed in the past few days. She was coming to see there were facets to the man she wouldn't have guessed at before.

He believed her.

She pressed a hand to her chest, to the warmth that blossomed there despite the lingering anxiety. Another man might have shrugged off her concerns, especially after witnessing firsthand one of her wild panic attacks.

But Jesse believed her.

Sarah lifted her face to the gloriously warm afternoon sun, wishing she didn't have to go back into her classroom in another few moments.

She would have been tempted to sacrifice her entire summer vacation if she could only spend the rest of the day right there on the playground with the sun on her face and that sweet-smelling breeze coyly teasing her hair and rustling her skirt around her legs.

She had spring fever as badly as her students. After a week of gloomy weather, she longed to be out in the garden, planting and pruning and fertilizing.

Who would have thought she would be so addicted to gardening? What had started out as a little thing earlier in the spring—a simple desire to plant a few flowers in the empty beds around the house—had quickly turned into an obsession.

It amazed her because it was so unexpected. She, who'd never even had a houseplant before, was turning into an avid gardener. She loved the whole process. Painstakingly selecting seeds or starts at the nursery, preparing the earth for them, watching the hesitant little green stalks slowly unfurl toward the sun.

There was an odd sense of power in the process. Though Mother Nature definitely played a heavy hand with her sun and rain, in all other respects Sarah was master of her little garden. She chose which seedlings belonged where, when and how many to plant, which to thin away and which would be given the chance to bloom.

She found it heady and intoxicating. At least in this one area of her life, she felt in control.

She rolled her eyes at herself—how pathetic was that?—then lifted her face to the sun.

On a day like this one, her panicked call to the police three nights earlier seemed unreal. Ridiculous. As far away as the few wispy clouds up there. She could only have been imagining that terrible moment when she thought she saw someone standing outside her back door. It was the only explanation that made any kind of sense.

This was Star Valley, a place that could practically be the poster child of peaceful, rural America.

Who here would want to lurk outside the house of a boring schoolteacher?

She sighed. No one. That's why she must have been imagining things.

Jesse had been very patient with her. He had been true to his word—several times each evening she had seen police vehicles drive past her house. She found their presence comforting. And if she carefully watched to see if a certain gorgeous police chief might be driving one of them, well, that was nobody's business but her own.

She glanced at her watch. Five more minutes before the bell. She hated to be a spoilsport, but she was going to have to start gathering her students. She glanced around the playground at the rope-jumping and the hopscotching and the heated game of four-square in the corner. The children looked jubilant to be outside. Maybe she could just hold class out in the sunshine today.

She spied Corey under the spreading branches of a maple tree whose leaves were small and new, his back propped against the trunk. As usual, he sat by himself, and her heart twisted with sympathy for him.

He had a few friends, she knew, but none in their class. Her students were not cruel to him, but they were uneasy around a boy with such a hostile attitude toward everything.

He could use some company, she decided, and ducked under the low overhang of branches to join him.

As she neared the boy, she could tell instantly something was wrong. Corey's head was buried in his arms and he was shivering slightly in the cool shade.

"Corey? Honey? Are you all right?"

After a long moment he lifted his face slowly, as if the movement pained him. He was pale, she saw with concern, his flushed cheeks the only spots of color on his face.

"I don't feel too good," he whispered.

She knelt in the grass and touched his forehead with her fingers. "You do seem warm. What else is going on?"

"My throat and my head hurt and I itch."

For the first time she noticed ominously familiar red blisters creeping up his neck and covering his arms below his sleeves.

"Where do you itch?"

He looked positively miserable. "Everywhere. Especially my stomach and my back."

"Oh, dear," she murmured.

Corey finally met her gaze, worry darkening his eyes. "What's wrong with me?"

For all his cocky bravado most of the time, he was still just a boy, she reminded herself. And right now he was a very sick boy. "Sweetheart, have you ever had the chicken pox?"

"No," he mumbled. "I don't think so."

"You do now."

The boy's eyes widened, his features twisted with dismay. "I can't. I'm supposed to help Chief Harte. We're supposed to practice today after school."

"He'll just have to do his presentation without you or reschedule it until you're better. You need to be home in bed. I'm sure that's what's itching. Let's take a look at your back."

She reached for his T-shirt. Corey froze, then scrambled back against the tree, out of her reach. "No. No. That's okay."

"Just pull it up a little so I can see how bad the spots are on your back."

He batted halfheartedly at her hands, but she persisted and finally lifted his T-shirt up just enough so she could see.

The normal playground noises around them—the rattle of chains on the swings, the shrieks and laughter of children, the breeze rustling the new maple leaves above them—seemed to fade away.

All she could hear was her own horrified gasp.

Halfway down his back, red, puckered skin surrounded a sickly gray scar in a distinctive S shape at least three inches long. It looked like a brand, like the ownership mark she saw on cows all around Wyoming.

Bile swelled in her throat and her stomach heaved. Dear Lord. How could anyone do such a thing to a child?

"Who did this to you?" she asked when she could find her voice through the horror.

His lips clamped together and he looked away from her, avoiding both her gaze and her question. Her hand shook, but she reached out anyway and gripped his shoulder firmly. Fury made her voice hard, tight. "Corey, answer me. Who did this?"

She felt him tremble a little under her fingers and realized she was taking completely the wrong tack with him. If her fierceness didn't scare him, it would only make him more belligerent. She yanked her hand back and shoved it into the pocket of her cardigan.

"Sweetheart, you have to tell me. This is wrong. Who did this to you?"

"Nobody," he finally answered. His voice sounded thin and raspy, but she didn't know if it was from fear or from his illness. "I...I did it myself."

She stared at him. "What?"

"Yeah. I did it. Well, I had my friend help."

Could he be telling the truth? She had read of children with severe emotional or developmental problems being self-destructive. Pounding their heads repeatedly against the cement or pulling out clumps of their hair or shredding their skin. She knew that sometimes physical pain could be a release valve of sorts for children who didn't know how else to cope with their emotional pain.

Maybe Corey was far more troubled than anybody realized.

Merciful heavens. Nothing in her training had prepared her for anything like this. She wanted to gather him into her arms and hold him close, but she didn't want to make a wrong move here. Perhaps she should leave this to trained professionals. But she cared about Corey too much.

"Why would you hurt yourself this way?" she asked quietly.

"Didn't burn much."

He was lying. She could see it in his eyes. It must have been excruciatingly painful—the scar still looked red and sore.

"Why, Corey?"

He shrugged, looking down at the grass. "My mom wouldn't let me get a tattoo."

"A...a tattoo?"

"I wanted my name but she said no, so I did an *S* for Sylvester."

"How?" Her voice sounded as raspy as his. "How did you do it?"

Corey still continued looking down at the grass. She looked at him carefully but couldn't tell if he was being evasive because he was embarrassed or because he was being less than honest.

"Me and some guys heard about gangs branding themselves. It sounded cool so we, um, decided to see if we could do it. We bent a hanger into an *S* and heated it up. You won't tell my mom, will you?"

Another wave of nausea washed through her. Dear heavens. The child was only ten years old and he was scarring himself, mutilating himself, to look cool. And then he was worried about her snitching to his mother!

The bell rang. She could see her students lining up at the door waiting to go in. They would have to do without her for a few more minutes, at least while she called Ginny Garrett. She would see if one of the other teachers could take her class until Corey's mother could arrive for him.

"You need to see a doctor, Corey."

"For the chicken pox?"

"And for your...for what you did. It could be infected."

"Then my mom and Seth would have to know."

"I can't keep this a secret, Corey. I'm sorry. It's not right. I have to tell them."

His face crumpled and again he looked exactly his age, like a scared little boy, then his features hardened into familiar belligerent lines. He called her a harsh name a ten-year-old had no business even knowing, let alone repeating. "You act like you're my friend, but you're not. You're just like all the other stupid teachers. If you tell my mom, you'll be sorry."

He climbed to his feet and would have run away, but she held him in place and half dragged him to the office so she could place the call. By the time they got inside the building, Corey stopped struggling. He walked along beside her like a prisoner on the way to Old Sparky.

Maybe Star Valley wasn't so idyllic after all, she thought as they neared the office. Not if children could do such horrible things to each other.

She didn't even want to think about the alternative, that someone else—his stepfather, maybe—might have done this to Corey.

Jesse pulled up to the Salt River Medical Clinic and sat in his Bronco, studying the low-slung cedar building. Ginny and Corey were still here. He could see her silver Range Rover in the parking lot.

Since Sarah's call a half hour earlier, the beauty of the bright April day seemed to have dimmed. The sun still shone, but its glow seemed tarnished somehow.

He muttered an oath. He could hardly believe what she'd told him—that Corey and his friends had branded themselves as if they were no better than cattle.

Sarah had been distressed almost to tears as she'd told him the details of the scar on Corey's back.

"It was horrible, Jesse. You should have seen him so calmly describing how he did it. I can't understand why he would do such a thing."

"It's not against the law, Sarah. I'd say this is something Ginny and Seth are going to have to deal with."

"I know. I just… You're going to think I'm crazy again, but when he was talking about it, I got the distinct impression he was lying about the circumstances. What if he didn't get it willingly? Couldn't criminal charges be filed then?"

"You think whoever might have given him those

black eyes and other injuries might be responsible for this, too?'' Jesse had asked.

''I don't know. Maybe.'' There had been a long silence on the other end, then Sarah had spoken quietly. ''I know you're busy, but will you please talk to him? Just see if you believe him. He's a child, Jesse. A boy who was squeamish last week when he skinned his knee on the playground. Why would he consent to do this to himself?''

In the end, what else could he do but agree to talk to the kid? Sarah trusted him to get to the bottom of the many mysteries surrounding the boy. How could he do anything else?

He blew out a breath and climbed out of the Bronco. Inside the clinic he found Ginny at the counter filling out insurance forms, bracing Maddie on her hip with one hand while she wrote with the other. She looked small and fragile.

Lost.

''Hey, Jesse,'' called Donna Jenkins, her red hair just a few shades lighter than her lipstick. The nurse gave him a flirtatious smile—the same one she always gave him—which he returned quickly before turning to Ginny.

''How did you find out?'' she asked, and he frowned at the defeated look in her eyes.

''Sarah—Ms. McKenzie—called me. She's worried about Corey.''

Ginny nodded, absently grabbing her baby's fingers before Maddie could steal the pen out of her hands.

''How is he?''

''He's in with Doc Wallace right now. He's definitely got the chicken pox, and the…the other thing is apparently infected. Doc Wallace is writing him a prescription for antibiotics.''

''You mind if I talk to him?''

She shrugged. ''You can try. He's not saying anything about it, but maybe you'll get more out of him than I can.''

Doc Wallace was just closing the door to the examination room when Jesse walked down the hallway. He turned in surprise when he saw him. ''Jesse Harte! What brings you here?''

Jesse could never see Salt River's crusty doctor without remembering that terrible night when he was seventeen and he'd been brought here right after the accident before being airlifted to the regional medical center in Salt Lake City. He had a flash of memory, of kind words and a comforting touch and teary blue eyes telling him without words that his parents hadn't made it.

He pushed the memory aside. ''I just wanted to have a word with your patient.''

''You really think this is a police matter? It seems to be just a boy doing something ridiculously stupid.''

''I'd still like to talk to him just to make sure.''

''I hope you've had the chicken pox, then. Just keep in mind he's a sick kid who might not be up to answering a lot of questions.''

Jesse nodded and pushed open the door. Corey was sitting on the exam table in a hospital robe, his scrawny legs dangling over the side. His eyes widened at the sight of Jesse, then narrowed in contempt and something else that looked like betrayal.

"She told you."

He played innocent. "Who?"

"Miss McKenzie. Why'd she have to go and tell you?"

"She was worried about you."

"The hell she is. She's just got it in for me like every other teacher."

"You know that's not true. She cares about you. If she didn't, I wouldn't be here."

"You gonna arrest me?"

"No. Nobody committed any crime here." He watched the boy carefully as he spoke. "Unless someone did this to you against your will. Do you know what that phrase means? Against your will?"

For just an instant, fear flashed through the boy's eyes, but he quickly looked down at his bare feet. "Yeah. It means if someone did something I didn't want them to do."

"Is that what happened?"

Corey's gaze darted around the examination room, to the sink and the door and the panda wallpaper. To anything but Jesse. "No," he finally said, his voice belligerent. "How many times do I have to say it? I wanted a tattoo and my mom wouldn't let me get one. I don't care what she says. I still think it's cool."

"What does your dad have to say about it?"

Again that fear tightened his features. "He...he didn't have anything to do with it."

For the first time, the boy's voice wavered and Jesse narrowed his eyes. Damn it. Could Sarah have been right about Seth all along? The thought made his stomach heave. "Corey, did your stepfather hurt you?"

Corey stared at him. "Seth? Hell, no. He wouldn't hurt me."

He looked so genuinely astonished at the suggestion that Jesse felt a vast relief. Seth was his friend. The idea that he might be involved in this was repugnant.

But if Seth didn't do it, who was hurting this child?

"I need some names, then."

That fear flashed across Corey's features again. "What names?"

"The other kids involved in this so I can make sure they get medical treatment if they need it."

Corey stuck out his chin. "I ain't tellin'."

"You don't want your friends getting sick, do you? You can die from a bad infection if it's not treated, did you know that? In the old days, before antibiotics, people died just from getting a cut in their finger."

He watched the wheels turning in the boy's head as he digested the information and considered his options. "The other guys chickened out," Corey finally said. "I was the only one with the stones to go through with it. Are you happy now?"

Not by a long shot. Sarah was right. There was far more to this than the boy was revealing in these crummy little bits and pieces.

"Why don't you give me their names anyway?" Jesse suggested. "Just so I can back up your story."

He crossed his arms and jutted his jaw. "No. I'm not squealing on my friends. Nothing you do is gonna change my mind."

Before Jesse could pressure him on it, the door opened and Doc Wallace entered, Ginny and Maddie right behind him.

"Everything okay in here?" Doc Wallace asked.

Jesse nodded. "We're just finishing up. Corey, think about what I said. If you decide to tell me anything else, either for your own safety or your friends' safety, you know how to get in touch with me, right?"

The boy managed a smirk, even though Jesse could tell he was miserable and itchy. "Yeah. But don't sit by the phone, 'cause I won't be callin'."

Jesse thought he would probably fall right off his chair if he ever did hear from the kid.

Chapter 8

Corey was the first of what turned into a virtual chicken pox epidemic at Salt River Elementary. In Sarah's class alone, six other children besides him had been hit with the nasty virus.

She sympathized with them all. She could still vividly remember her own awful bout with chicken pox when she was eight—the itching and the sore, swollen throat and the unrelenting tedium of being quarantined at home for ten days.

Her professor parents had juggled their respective class loads so one of them could be home with her during the day, but even the rarity of being completely at the center of their attention hadn't been enough to make up for the misery.

The boredom had been the worst, she remembered. Knowing how energetic her students had been, she figured they were all going crazy being cooped up while spring exploded around them.

The night before, she had come up with the idea of delivering care packages for her poor students, complete with a few books, word puzzles and games to keep their minds off the torment.

She had to admit, a big part of her motivation for the visits to her students was a desire to make amends with Corey. She knew he still hadn't forgiven her for telling his mother and Jesse about the crude *S* branded onto his back.

Her peace offering had been in vain, though. He wouldn't even allow his mother to let Sarah into his bedroom, so she'd ended up dropping his package off with Ginny.

Corey was the first stop. The rest of her Saturday morning had been much more rewarding. The children had been as delighted to have a visit at home from their teacher as they were about the books and small gifts.

She smiled, remembering the joy on all their dearly familiar little faces. What would she have done if she'd given in to her impulse right after the attack and left teaching? She would have missed it beyond measure. She needed her students to bring laughter and innocence into her life.

Well, most of them were innocent. Her thoughts returned full circle to Corey. She had to find another way to reach him, but she didn't have the first clue where to start.

She pushed the troubling thoughts away and concentrated on the drive. What a lousy day to be sick, she thought again as she cruised along the winding road toward her last stop, the Diamond Harte—hit with the double whammy of both Dylan and Lucy coming down with the spots.

The day was sunny and warm, with only a few high,

powder-puff clouds to break up the vast blue expanse of sky.

Springtime in the Rockies was glorious, she was discovering. Snow still capped the highest peaks, but everything else burst with lush, vibrant color. She loved seeing evidence of new life everywhere, from the lambs leaping in pastures to the new leaves on the trees to the buds erupting everywhere in her garden.

And the road to the Diamond Harte was among the prettiest she'd traveled in Star Valley. A creek tumbled beside it, full and swift from runoff. Lining the banks were sturdy cottonwoods, thick green undergrowth and the occasional stunning red stalks she'd learned were a western relative of the more common southern dogwood.

On the other side of the creek, in a pasture surrounded by gleaming white fences, a trio of horses raced against her trusty little Toyota as it climbed the last hill before the ranch house.

At the crest, she stopped for a moment to savor the view.

The Diamond Harte nestled in a small, verdant valley. At the center was the ranch house itself, a sprawling log-and-stone structure that looked as if it had been there forever.

It was flanked by a huge red barn and a half dozen other outbuildings. More of those beautiful, sleek horses grazed in pastures here and she remembered that Matt Harte, Jesse's brother, raised not only cattle but champion cutting horses.

This was where Jesse had grown to manhood. He had probably climbed those fences and raced bareback across those fields of green and floated twig boats down the creek.

She felt a strange little tug at her heart picturing the big, gorgeous man who both terrified and intrigued her as a mischievous boy with startling blue eyes and a devil's grin.

Drat. Couldn't she even go fifteen minutes without thinking of him? She hadn't talked to him since the week before, the day she had seen Corey's stomach, and she hated to admit that she missed him. The way those blue eyes crinkled at the corners when he smiled, the funny little flutter in her stomach whenever he looked at her, the way he somehow always managed to tease her out of her nervousness.

He was so vibrant and alive, he made her world seem much more drab in contrast.

She had to stop this. Firmly pushing thoughts of Jesse away, she drove the rest of the way to the ranch house, then carried her bags up the porch steps and rang the doorbell.

Ellie Webster Harte—Star Valley's busiest veterinarian—answered the door.

Ellie always seemed so beautiful and together whenever Sarah saw her. Today, though, her hair was slipping from a ponytail, she didn't have any makeup on and the T-shirt she wore had a streak of flour dusting one shoulder. She looked frazzled and worn-out.

"Sarah!" she exclaimed. "Matt told me you called and were on your way out. What a brave soul you are to face our miserable pair!"

Sarah smiled. She had come to know Ellie earlier in the year when they'd worked together on a school fund-raising project and she genuinely liked the other woman.

Though they had arrived in Salt River at roughly the

same time, that was about the only similarity between them.

Ellie was spunky and energetic and not at all afraid to go after what she wanted—everything Sarah used to be. She had often marveled at the courage Ellie must have had to uproot her daughter and move to Star Valley, away from everything that was familiar.

"How are the girls?" she asked.

Ellie made a face. "Awful. We've already given them each two oatmeal baths and smeared them with calamine and they're still itching like crazy. Give me a whole stable full of sick horses any day over two nine-year-olds with chicken pox. They're climbing the walls."

Sarah laughed and held up the gift bags she'd packed. "Maybe these will help entertain them, at least for an hour or so."

"You're an angel! I can't believe you went to so much trouble!"

"It was no trouble. I love the girls. I just wish I could do more to help them feel better."

Before the other woman could answer, the smell of burnt chocolate wafted out of the kitchen.

Ellie sniffed, then her face dropped. "Rats!" she moaned. "My cookies! I have to confess, I'm not much of a cook. That's Cassie's expertise. But the girls were craving chocolate chip, so I did my best. I swear, we'd all starve if Cassie wasn't bringing regular meals over from the Lost Creek."

"I'll run these up to the girls while you rescue your cookies, okay?"

"Thanks. Third door at the top of the stairs." Ellie rushed down the hall toward the kitchen, leaving Sarah standing alone in the entry.

Her knee burned a little by the time she made it up the long flight of stairs, but she ignored it as she counted doors. Even without Ellie's directions, she would have known the third door on the right belonged to the girls by the collage of teen idols whose faces plastered the door.

She smiled a little as she pushed it open, then her heart seemed to stutter in her chest and she stopped breathing.

Jesse Harte, the subject of way too many of her thoughts lately, sprawled at the foot of one of the two twin beds in the room. Dylan and Lucy sat together at the other end wearing matching flannel pajamas. All three of them held playing cards, and other cards were scattered across the bedspread.

Jesse obviously hadn't been expecting her, but his surprise quickly gave way to a grin of delighted welcome. He opened his mouth to greet her, but the girls had caught sight of her first and beat him to the punch.

As usual, Dylan was the first to speak. "Miss McKenzie!" she exclaimed. "What are you doing here?"

There was that flutter in her stomach again as Jesse grinned at her. Sarah tried fiercely to ignore it, just as she usually ignored the nagging ache in her knee. She held up the matching pink gift bags. "I brought treats."

The girls shrieked and dived over their uncle toward the bags.

"Oh, sure." He gave a rueful laugh that did funny little things to her nerve endings. "This is the thanks I get for spending two solid hours listening to your boy band music and letting you both whip my butt at crazy eights. The minute a pretty lady walks into the room carrying presents, you both forget all about me."

The girls looked back at their uncle, clearly torn about what was the most polite thing to do in this situation, until Jesse rolled his eyes at them. "I'm joking. Go ahead. I know you're dying to see what goodies Miz McKenzie brought for you."

They gleefully dived for the bags again and the next few moments were filled with ripping paper and exclamations of delight.

Their enthusiasm made her smile as she watched them, grateful for whatever impulse had given her the idea for the gift bags.

Out of the corner of her gaze, she sneaked a peek at Jesse. She expected him to be looking at his nieces, too, but to her astonishment, his attention was focused only on her.

"That was a very nice thing to do, Miz McKenzie," he murmured. The approval in his blue eyes slid through her like a caress, completely disarming her.

"It's not much. Nothing compared to two hours of crazy eights and all the pop music you can stand."

"I am feeling a little unhinged right about now. I never realized there were so many ways for teenage boys who can't even grow chest hair yet to sing about losing the loves of their pitiful young lives."

She listened to the sounds emanating from a small shelf CD player and had to smile. "I heard this particular group is coming in concert to Idaho Falls next month," she teased. "Since you love their music so much, maybe you should take the girls."

She hadn't meant Dylan and Lucy to overhear, but unfortunately the chicken pox hadn't affected their hearing at all.

"Yes!" Lucy gasped with astonished joy. "Oh, Uncle Jess, that would be so awesome! Please, please, please?''

He glared at Sarah. "Thank you very much. Now how am I supposed to get out of it?''

She fought the urge to clamp a hand over her mouth, dismayed that her teasing Jesse had begun to spiral out of control. It would have been too late, anyway. The damage was already done.

"Sorry," she whispered to Jesse.

"If I have to go, you're coming with me," he growled back.

Although he sounded disgruntled, she could see by the glint in his blue eyes that he wasn't really upset. Relief washed over her. She wasn't sure she could handle having this man angry with her.

"I'm sure I probably have plans that day," she assured him.

"Break them. You're not getting out of this that easily—you're coming with us.''

"Does that mean we're really going?" Lucy asked gleefully.

"I guess you both do have birthdays coming up. I'll have to see if I can swing tickets for the four of us," he answered, with a pointed look at Sarah.

For the next few moments the girls could talk of nothing else but their favorite group, until Sarah felt her eyes begin to glaze over. She was out of her depth here.

But even though she knew she had no real excuse for staying, Sarah couldn't make herself walk out the door, too busy watching and listening to the camaraderie between Jesse and his nieces.

The girls obviously adored him. Sarah was ashamed to discover she was jealous of their bond. The glaring contrast between Jesse's boisterous family and her own solitary life depressed her, made her feel even more alone.

She was just about to make her excuses and leave when Ellie walked into the room in time to catch the girls yawning in tandem.

"I saw that," Ellie said with a frown. "Ladies, it appears your uncle and Miss McKenzie have tired you right out."

"It's exhausting business whipping me at every hand. Isn't that right?"

Even tired, Dylan could still serve up a cheeky grin. "Not really. We're used to it by now."

"Be that as it may," her mother said sternly, "I think you'll both feel better after you rest for a while."

The girls groaned as Jesse climbed to his feet. "Well, Miz McKenzie, I believe that's our cue to leave these two card sharks to their beds."

"Matt said you planned to ride the Piñon trail this afternoon," Ellie said to him as she tucked the girls in. "How far do you think you'll make it? Before he took off for Afton this morning, your brother said to warn you the snow levels were still pretty deep a few weeks ago when he was up there and you might not make it very high."

Jesse's grin was every bit as cheeky as Dylan's. "Doesn't matter, as long as I'm far enough to get out of range of the cell phone. It's my day off, but Lou doesn't seem to know what that means. She still calls me a dozen times a day."

"Didn't it ever occur to you to simply turn your phone off?" Sarah asked.

"What's the challenge in that? Besides, I could

never lie to Lou if she asked why she couldn't reach me. This way I don't have to.''

He glanced at her, a considering look in his blue eyes. "Do you ride?"

"Um, horses?"

"No. African elephants. Of course, horses."

The girls giggled and Sarah smiled, amazed that she enjoyed his teasing so much. "Not really. I know the front end of a horse from the back, but that's about it. I think the last time I rode was probably at summer camp the year I turned twelve."

"Doesn't matter. We can give you one of the more gentle horses and take it slow."

She didn't like the sound of that "we" business. "I don't really think…"

"What a great idea!" Ellie exclaimed. "Sarah, you have to go with him. It's such a gorgeous day, you'd be crazy not to."

"You can take my horse or Dylan's," Lucy chimed in. "Dandy and Speck are both really gentle."

Confronted with four Harte faces watching her with the same eager expression, Sarah knew she was well and truly trapped. She tried in vain to come up with a polite way to decline the invitation without disappointing them all.

She couldn't very well tell them the prospect terrified her. Not riding a horse up a mountain trail on a beautiful spring day—she had to admit she found that idea thrilling and adventurous, in keeping with the way she was trying to repair her life.

Riding that horse alone with Jesse Harte was another story, though.

She had come a long way in conquering her nervousness around him, but the idea of spending an hour or two alone in his company was as daunting as sky-diving with her bum knee.

"You're completely outnumbered," Jesse finally said with that same devastating grin. "Only way you'll get out of it now is to come down with the chicken pox yourself."

"Unfortunately, I've already had them, so I'm immune," she murmured.

"Too bad. Guess that means you'll have to go with me, then." His grin just about took her breath away.

With a resigned sigh, she followed him out into the hallway, wishing fiercely that she'd been smart enough to build up an immunity to a certain police chief she could name.

He shouldn't have railroaded her into this.

Jesse watched Sarah duck her head to ride under a thick, fringy pine branch spreading over the trail. A few drops of rain from the quick shower the night before still nestled among the needles. As she brushed under it and emerged on the other side, glistening droplets clung to her thick blond hair like stars.

No, he definitely shouldn't have brought her. Not because she wasn't enjoying it. On the contrary. Her eyes shone as brightly as the water droplets in the sunlight and her face beamed with excitement.

He shouldn't have brought her because he didn't need to see this side of her. He didn't *want* to see it. It was tough enough fighting this completely inappropriate attraction to her in town, when she was shy and nervous around him. This smiling, glowing woman was damn near impossible to resist.

But he would resist her. He had to.

He had already worked hard to convince himself that

he had to keep a safe, casual distance between them. She wasn't his type. He had a strict policy against becoming involved with breakable women and he had the feeling Sarah was more fragile than most.

On the other side of the trees, the trail widened enough for two horses. He dug his heels into his horse's side and caught up with her.

"You're doing great. How's your knee?"

"A little achy, but nothing out of the ordinary."

He wondered again how she had injured it. A car accident? A sports injury, maybe? Somehow he didn't think so. Call it cop's intuition, but he had a feeling her injured knee had some connection with whatever put those shadows in her pretty green eyes.

He also knew she wasn't about to share that information with him.

"Maybe we better not push it. We can stop just up ahead. There's a spot up there where you can see the whole valley."

They climbed one last rise in the trail, to a wide plateau covered in meadow grass and piles of melting snow. He helped her dismount and the two of them walked closer to the edge, toward a handful of large granite rocks. She perched on one and wrapped her arms around her knees as she gazed in wonder at the panoramic view.

"This is incredible! I didn't realize we were climbing so high. I swear, you can see clear to Jackson Hole!"

He leaned a hip against the boulder. "Not quite. If we went all the way to the top of the trail, we could."

"It's so gorgeous, it almost makes me want to cry."

He smiled at her awestruck expression. "Please don't! I'm not very good with crying women."

"I imagine you're probably good with any kind of women," she muttered under her breath, so low he thought he must have been mistaken.

He decided he would probably be wise to change the subject. "There's the Diamond Harte." He pointed to the ranch. "Prettiest spot in the valley, isn't it?"

"How big is the ranch?"

"About ten thousand acres, give or take a few. Then we have grazing rights to about that same number on Forest Service land above the ranch. In a month or so when the snow melts a little more, I'll be taking a couple days off to help Matt and his men drive them up there. It's a great time. If you're around, you ought to come out and watch."

He turned and found her watching him, her eyes soft and a small smile lifting the edges of her mouth the way the breeze fluttered the ends of her hair. "You love the ranch, don't you?"

She was so beautiful. He swallowed hard, fighting down the sudden fierce urge to reach for her. Finally he had to look away from her and back down at the place he'd been raised.

"Yeah," he finally said. "Yeah, I do love it."

"Why didn't you stay?"

How could he answer that? Jesse gazed down at the ranch and then over at the town sprawled just a few miles away from it, acutely aware of the wind rattling the aspens and the quiet fluttering of insects around them and the vast, beautiful silence of the mountainside.

He thought of several things at the same time. His parents' deaths, the reckless, selfish choices he'd made in the intervening years. The debt he owed to the people of Star Valley who had been willing to forgive.

Finally he shrugged. "Ranching was Matt's dream, not mine. I was too restless to be happy at it for long."

"What was your dream?"

He smiled ruefully. It had taken him years to figure that out. "I wanted to be on the right side of the law for a change. I love putting on that badge every morning and knowing today might be the day I save someone's life or return someone's property or help someone find lost hope again."

She was watching him again with that warm light in her eyes. Damn, he wished she wouldn't do that. "You're a good person, Jesse Harte."

"Don't kid yourself, Miz McKenzie," he murmured.

Badge or not, he was still the bad boy of Salt River and always would be. There was one sure way to prove it, he thought, and leaned across the space between them, toward that softly curving mouth.

He shouldn't be doing this. The thought registered briefly, but he didn't heed it. He had been itching to kiss her for too long. He wasn't about to give up this chance, even though he knew it was a mistake.

An instant later, his mouth brushed hers and he forgot everything but her.

Sarah froze. Her breath lodged somewhere in the vicinity of her throat and she was vaguely aware of a wild fluttering of her pulse.

He was going to kiss her. She could tell by the way he angled his head, by the sudden glittery light in his eyes.

She wanted to tell him to stop. She wanted to cry out that he shouldn't waste his time kissing her.

That she was broken.

But she couldn't hang on to any of those thoughts

fluttering through her head like drab moths. Not when his beautiful, rugged features were only inches away, when she could feel the soft caress of his breath on her cheek.

She wanted him to kiss her, she realized with shock. She wanted to feel those hard, beautiful lips on hers, to taste his mouth, to know the sweet edge of passion once again.

Was that the fragile sensation sparkling to life inside her? Desire? She barely recognized the feeling, it had been so very long since she'd experienced it. She had begun to fear maybe that was just one more part of her that had shriveled up and blown away after the attack.

But no. Desire was definitely seeping through her bones, settling in all the deep, empty hollows inside her.

She wanted Jesse Harte to kiss her. Wanted it fiercely, so fiercely it was stronger even than the thin sliver of fear curling through her.

He paused for just an instant and watched her out of those incredible blue eyes, and then his mouth dipped to hers.

Please don't let me panic. Please don't let me panic, she prayed.

Her heart stuttered briefly, but the instant his mouth brushed hers, she forgot all about being afraid.

He had obviously kissed a lot of women. He knew just the right way to skim his lips against hers, to make her feel wanted and needed, not overpowered.

She sighed into his mouth and closed her eyes to savor every moment. The masculine smell of him—a heady, woodsy mix of pine and sage and leather—his warm mouth that tasted like chocolate peppermints, the slight rasp of stubble against her skin.

Sensation after sensation poured over her and she wanted it to go on forever. Her position on the boulder put them at about the same height and she found it easy for her hands to creep around his neck, for her to draw him closer so she could continue to lose herself to the wonder of his mouth.

She wanted this man. Those first trickles of tentative desire swelled and surged with each touch of his mouth, until they rushed through her like spring runoff, pooling in her womb, between her thighs, in her heart. Until she wanted to weep with a vast, wonderful relief.

She wanted him! It seemed like a miracle, like rediscovering a part of herself she'd thought was lost forever.

His tongue licked at the corners of her mouth and she parted her lips, welcoming him inside. The kiss deepened and she could feel heat emanating from him like a sun-warmed rock.

She wanted everything, wanted those hard arms around her and his hair under her fingers and his hands on her skin. She made a soft noise in her throat and pulled him closer.

At the sound she made, Jesse froze and pulled back. Talk about a plan backfiring. He tried fiercely to catch his breath, to hang on to the last shreds of control.

He'd meant to show her he was too wild for a woman like her. Maybe scare her a little so she'd stop looking at him with those damn stars in her eyes.

So much for that idea.

She had stunned him.

That was the only word for it. He couldn't remember ever feeling as completely undone by a woman, by the torrent of emotions that single kiss had sent tumbling through him—tenderness and protectiveness and a raw, hot need.

He wanted to pull her close, to safeguard her from whatever sometimes put that lost look in her eyes, to keep her safe and warm and loved.

Now he was the one who was scared to death. Breathing hard, he shoved his hands into his pockets and was amazed—and even more terrified—to realize they were shaking slightly.

It was just a kiss.

He'd kissed plenty of women before, tasted their mouths, touched their skin. Too many, according to Matt and Cassie. They liked to teasingly accuse him of leaving a long string of bruised and broken hearts across western Wyoming.

They were wrong. He had hurt a few women, he hated to admit it, but not on purpose. He had always made it abundantly clear up front to the women he dated that he wasn't looking for anything permanent.

Most of the time, that's all they wanted, too—he was careful to make sure of that—but one or two had started to take things too seriously.

When he could see them getting that light in their eyes that warned him they were starting to dream of wedding cakes and flower girls, he knew it was time to break things off.

He liked party girls. He wasn't ashamed to admit it. Big hair, big smiles, big breasts. Maybe it was a hold-over from his wild younger days. He didn't drink any-more, didn't smoke, didn't swear much, but he still liked to date women who knew how to have a good time. Women who were there only for the short term.

So what was he thinking to kiss Sarah McKenzie— a very long-term kind of woman—as if he meant it?

And why, if it was just a kiss, did he feel as if that boulder she was sitting on had just rolled right over him?

He blew out a breath and sneaked a look at her. Big mistake. Her eyes were all soft and dewy and she almost looked as if she was going to tear up any minute now.

Panic ripped through him. He couldn't bear it when women cried.

What the hell was he supposed to do now?

He'd blown it big-time and now he was going to have to work even harder to keep away from her. A soft, fragile, forever kind of woman like Sarah McKenzie deserved far better than a rough lawman with wild blood running through his veins.

Trouble was, he didn't *want* to stay away from her. He liked her, respected her and—damn his hide—still wanted her.

He cleared his throat. "Should we keep going up the trail or are you ready to head back?"

She blinked at him, looking more vulnerable than a tiny kitten in the middle of a pack of junkyard dogs, and he watched her trying to gather her composure. Little by little, that glowing color began to fade from her face. He told himself he was relieved, but a hard kernel of regret dug into his heart as he watched it disappear.

"I…maybe we'd better head back," she murmured. "It's later than I realized and I have some things to do back in town."

He nodded and brought the horses over, then tried to make as little contact with her as possible while helping her into the saddle, afraid that if he touched

Silhouette ROMANCE® 1444
$3.50 U.S.
$3.99 CAN
MR/

DIANA PALMER

MERCENARY'S WOMAN
SOLDIERS OF FORTUNE

We'd like to send you **2 FREE** books and a surprise gift to introduce you to Silhouette Intimate Moments®.
Accept our special offer today and
Get Ready for a totally Refreshing Experience!

HOW TO QUALIFY:

1. With a coin, carefully scratch off the silver area on the card at right to see what we have for you—2 FREE BOOKS and a FREE GIFT—ALL YOURS! ALL FREE!

2. Send back the card and you'll receive two brand-new Silhouette Intimate Moments® novels. These books have a cover price of $4.50 each in the U.S. and $5.25 each in Canada, but they are yours to keep absolutely free!

3. There's no catch. You're under no obligation to buy anything. We charge nothing— ZERO—for your first shipment and you don't have to make any minimum number of purchases—not even one!

4. The fact is, thousands of readers enjoy receiving books by mail from the Silhouette Reader Service®. They enjoy the convenience of home delivery…they like getting the best new novels at discount prices, BEFORE they're available in stores…and they love their *Heart to Heart* subscriber newsletter featuring author news, horoscopes, recipes, book reviews and much more!

5. We hope that after receiving your free books you'll want to remain a subscriber. But the choice is yours—to continue or cancel, any time at all. So why not take us up on our invitation with no risk of any kind. You'll be glad you did!

SPECIAL FREE GIFT!

We can't tell you what it is…but we're sure you'll like it! A FREE gift just for giving the Silhouette Reader Service® a try!

Visit us at
www.eHarlequin.com

The **2 FREE BOOKS** we send you will be selected from **SILHOUETTE INTIMATE MOMENTS**®, the series that brings you...fast-paced romantic adventure and excitement.

Books received may vary.

2 FREE BOOKS and a FREE GIFT!

Scratch off the silver area to see what the Silhouette Reader Service has for you.

Silhouette®
Where love comes alive™

YES!

I have scratched off the silver area above. Please send me the **2 FREE** books and gift for which I qualify. I understand I am under no obligation to purchase any books, as explained on the back and on the opposite page.

345 SDL DH5E   **245 SDL DH5D**

FIRST NAME   LAST NAME

ADDRESS

APT.#   CITY

STATE/PROV.   ZIP/POSTAL CODE

Offer limited to one per household and not valid to current Silhouette Intimate Moments® subscribers. All orders subject to approval.

THE SILHOUETTE READER SERVICE®—Here's how it works:

Accepting your 2 free books and gift places you under no obligation to buy anything. You may keep the books and gift and return the shipping statement marked "cancel." If you do not cancel, about a month later we'll send you 6 additional books and bill you just $3.80 each in the U.S., or $4.21 each in Canada, plus 25¢ shipping & handling per book and applicable taxes if any.* That's the complete price and — compared to cover prices of $4.50 each in the U.S. and $5.25 each in Canada — it quite a bargain! You may cancel at any time, but if you choose to continue, every month we'll send you 6 more books, which you may either purchase at the discount price or return to us and cancel your subscription.

*Terms and prices subject to change without notice. Sales tax applicable in N.Y. Canadian residents will be charged applicable provincial taxes and GST.

If offer card is missing write to: Silhouette Reader Service, 3010 Walden Ave., P.O. Box 1867, Buffalo NY 14240-1867

DETACH AND MAIL CARD TODAY!

BUSINESS REPLY MAIL
FIRST-CLASS MAIL   PERMIT NO. 717-003   BUFFALO, NY

POSTAGE WILL BE PAID BY ADDRESSEE

SILHOUETTE READER SERVICE
3010 WALDEN AVE
PO BOX 1867
BUFFALO NY 14240-9952

NO POSTAGE
NECESSARY
IF MAILED
IN THE
UNITED STATES

any more of that soft skin, he might pull her into his arms and not let go.

The ride down the trail was uncomfortable, stiff and quiet. The birds were still singing, the mountains still bright and cheerful with spring, but much of the joy seemed to have gone out of the day.

All too soon, they arrived back at the Diamond Harte. He reined in near the ranch house, then went to help her dismount. She felt small and fragile in his hands—his fingers almost touched around her waist.

He released her quickly before he could pull her back into his arms. Maybe he moved *too* quickly. When he helped her to the ground, she stumbled a little and he had to reach for her again to steady her.

"I'm okay," she assured him, stepping away. "Just a little wobbly."

"Are you sure?"

"Yes. Thank you for taking me," she said brightly. Too brightly. "I didn't realize how much I've missed riding."

He had hurt her. He could tell by the brittleness in her voice and the distance in her eyes. Damn. That's what he'd been afraid of.

"I'm sure Matt would let you ride his horses any-time you'd like. There are dozens of trails above the ranch that are perfect for an hour or two trail ride. I'll talk to him about it for you if you'd like."

Her smile looked as if one of the girls had stuck it on her face with glue, but missed the corners somehow. "I appreciate the offer, but when I want to ride again, I'll talk to him. Thanks anyway. Do you need help putting the horses up?"

They were talking like polite strangers, like distant,

formal acquaintances, and he hated it. "No. I've got it."

"Well, goodbye then. Thank you again."

"Sarah…" *I'm sorry,* he started to say. She looked at him expectantly but he wasn't sure exactly what he was apologizing for. For kissing her? Or for stopping?

"Never mind," he mumbled.

She pursed her lips, gave him one more of those terrible imitations of her smile, then walked to her car with her limp just a little more pronounced than usual.

What had she been thinking?

She should never have climbed on the back of that horse the day before, should never have gone riding with Jesse.

With every muscle in her body aching, Sarah stepped away from the bulletin board she was redecorating in her classroom Sunday evening. She gingerly eased onto the softest chair she could find in the room—one of the rolling computer chairs that, to her everlasting relief, possessed a comfortably padded seat.

She was going to be here all night trying to finish this thing if she had to continue taking these breaks every ten minutes.

The breaks had become a necessity, though. She stretched her knee out carefully and winced at the hot ache that forcefully reminded her of her folly. Unfortunately, her knee wasn't the only sore part of her body, but it seemed to have borne the worst of it.

She refused to acknowledge the other, not-so-physical ache that had settled somewhere in the vicinity of her heart after her afternoon spent with Jesse Harte.

She refused to regret their kiss, her aching heart notwithstanding. It had been warm and soft and sexy, and had made her feel wonderfully alive for the first time in months.

What she *did* regret—no matter how much time she spent castigating herself for the futility of it—was that she would never have the chance to kiss him again.

Jesse had made it clear he wouldn't be kissing her again anytime soon. He had ridden down the mountainside as if he had a snarling grizzly at his back.

The irony had not escaped her. For so long she had believed she would never feel desire again, never want to be with any man again.

And when she suddenly discovered that part of her hadn't died, had only been lurking somewhere deep inside, the man she wanted was obviously not interested.

She had to stop thinking about him. Mooning over the man wasn't helping her finish the job here.

She sighed and forced her attention back to the bulletin board, with its border of smiling suns wearing dark glasses, a not-so-subtle reminder that summer was just around the corner.

This would be her last bulletin board of the school year, since the term ended in just a few weeks.

Would she be here in the fall to take this one down and put up a new one, to greet a new crowd of fourth graders with their shiny notebooks and stiff new blue jeans and unsharpened pencils?

She hadn't decided yet. When she came to Star Valley, she had signed only a one-year contract, subject to renegotiation at the end of the school year. She had yet to make up her mind about signing a new one and teaching here another year.

On the one hand, Star Valley had provided exactly what she had needed the past nine months. Peace and safety. A place to regroup, to find the strength to survive.

A place to heal.

On the other hand, she feared she was becoming too comfortable here. Was she hiding out from the realities of the world in this place where she lived most of her life alone?

Maybe it was time to go back to Chicago. Maybe she would never really feel herself again—or at least finally begin to like the woman she had become—until she returned to face her friends and her family and her nightmare.

She didn't have to decide this tonight. She stapled the last smiling sun on the border, then stepped back to admire her work. Perfect. Now she could go home and soak her loudly complaining muscles in a nice hot bath.

She was cleaning up the mess she had made when she heard it.

A scratching, skittery sound that didn't belong in the quiet of her classroom.

Her heart gave a couple of hard knocks in her chest and she couldn't move. She could feel the flashback hovering on the edge of her consciousness. Broken glass. Hurtful hands. Choking, paralyzing terror.

Just before it claimed her, she realized with a vast, painful relief what had made the sound. Only a branch from the maple tree outside her window dancing in the cool spring breeze.

The problem was, she'd seen entirely too many horror movies when she was younger, too many shows where a scratching at the window turned out to be something far less benign than the wind.

"Scaredy-cat," she chided herself, breathing hard to force oxygen back into her bloodstream.

Being alone in the school had always spooked her a little, even before Tommy DeSilva. Sometimes she could swear she heard the distant echo of children's laughter, the rapping of a ruler on a desk.

And, thanks to him, now she heard phantom attackers lurking around every corner.

She hated being afraid.

Maybe that's why she forced herself to come to her classroom so often on the weekend or in the evening. To demystify it. Maybe if she spent enough time here, she would eventually become inured to the bumps and squeaks, to the branches scraping against her window.

Or maybe she just wanted to torture herself.

Whatever the reason, her psyche had had quite enough for tonight. Sarah shrugged into her fleece jacket, then turned off her light and quickly walked outside.

She felt instantly better out in the fresh air. The night was crisp, the breeze sweet and clean. A perfect spring night to follow two beautiful days. Above the lights of town, moonlight gleamed on the snow-covered peaks of the Salt River range standing solid and firm.

How could she leave here? She had come to love everything about Star Valley, through all the changing seasons.

She couldn't leave, despite her suddenly awkward relationship with Jesse Harte. She wanted to be here in August when the students came back, she wanted to take up Nordic skiing next winter if her knee would allow it, she wanted to ride the Piñon trail again and feel the cool mountain air on her face.

She would tell Chuck Hendricks on Monday that she

would sign the contract and return for another year. She wasn't hiding away here. She was building a new life for herself.

She was smiling—and favoring her knee only a little, she was pleased to discover—when she turned onto Spruce Street and passed old Mrs. Jensen's cow-shaped mailbox.

The riot of tulips lining her neighbor's wrought-iron fence swayed in the breeze, their colors ghostly pale under the soft moonlight, and Sarah stopped for a moment to admire them.

She would bury tulip bulbs this fall, she decided. Masses of them, in every conceivable color. Reds, pinks, yellows, purples. And next spring she would wait eagerly for them to poke through the earth.

Already sketching out in her mind where she would plant them all—and daffodils, too—she was still smiling as she reached her own mailbox and started up the walk.

She was halfway to the porch when she lifted her head and saw it.

The porch light was still burning—she had turned it on when she left, as she always did when she expected to be home after dark—and its glow illuminated a scene that looked as if it belonged in one of those horror movies she'd been thinking about earlier.

Chapter 9

Jesse's cellular phone bleated just as the Utah Jazz basketball team tied the score at the end of the fourth quarter, pushing the critical postseason game into overtime.

So much for enjoying the last few hours of his time off.

He groaned and glared at the phone. His efforts to convince some of his officers they could handle all but the most urgent crises without him didn't seem to be working. They still called to check with him before making almost any kind of decision, from whether to give tickets or warnings to first-time traffic offenders to what kind of coffee filters worked best in the machine.

He'd have to work a little harder, apparently.

"This better be good," he growled into the phone.

Silence met his snarl, then a small, ragged-sounding voice spoke. "Jesse? Is that you?"

He forgot the basketball game in an instant as cold fear clawed at him. "Sarah! What's wrong?" He knew instinctively that she wouldn't have used this number unless absolutely necessary, especially not after the awkwardness of the day before on the mountain.

"Can you… Do you think you could come over?"

He shoved into his boots, not taking the time to bother with socks. "I'm already heading for the door."

"I'm sorry to bother you. I didn't know who else to call."

She sounded strange, disoriented, almost as if she was high on something, but he knew that was impossible. She couldn't be using. Not sweet, fragile Sarah McKenzie.

He remembered the day she had freaked out on her back porch when her knee gave out and he'd reached to keep her from falling. That's the way she seemed now—like someone on the verge of a full-blown panic attack.

"What's going on?" he asked, trying to tamp down on his own panic.

"I don't know. There's blood everywhere. Please hurry."

Blood. Everywhere. Those were the only words that registered.

"Sarah?" he called into the phone, but the line went dead. In an instant, he yanked his sidearm from the closet and raced for his Bronco, calling for an ambulance and backup as he went.

He drove the six blocks to her house with all his lights flashing and siren blaring, and broke just about every traffic law on the Salt River books—and a few the city council hadn't had a chance to come up with yet.

On Spruce Street he braked hard and the Bronco shuddered to a stop just a few feet from where she stood in the middle of the road, clutching a cell phone and rocking back and forth on her heels.

He jumped from the truck and rushed to her, pulling her into his arms. "Sarah! What happened? Sit down. Where are you hurt?"

"No. It's not me."

He was so completely focused on her—on trying to visually assess her injuries—that he wasn't aware of anything else until she pointed toward her house. "There."

Reluctant to take his eyes off her for even a moment, he turned with impatience in the direction she was pointing. At first he didn't know what he was seeing. It just looked like dark shadows where there shouldn't be any, smears of muddy black.

Then his gaze sharpened and he realized what he was seeing.

His jaw sagged and he hissed a disbelieving curse, horrified by the scene. The dark shadows weren't shadows at all but blood. And, as she had whispered into the phone, it was everywhere.

On her porch pillars, on the door, pooled on her steps. Quarts of it. Buckets. It looked as if someone had butchered a cow right at her front door.

What in the world?

He stared, trying to comprehend it. He'd been a cop for a dozen years, had investigated everything from car accidents to bar fights to spouse abuse—and even a murder a few years back when one ranch hand had shot another over a woman.

But he couldn't remember ever seeing anything this grisly.

It couldn't possibly be hers. She wouldn't still be standing if it were. As if on cue, at just that moment she seemed to wobble in his arms. Even if she wasn't injured, he realized, she was shocky. Her face was pale as death in the moonlight, she was shaking uncontrollably and she looked as if she would fall over at the first stiff wind.

"Let's get you into the Bronco." He picked her up, struck by how delicate she felt in his arms, then settled her into the passenger seat. He had a wool blanket in the back in case of emergencies, although in his wildest dreams he would never have come up with this kind of scenario. He reached for it and tucked it around her.

"Can you tell me what happened?" he asked.

She shrugged helplessly. "I don't know. I was at the school working...."

"This late? By yourself?"

At the fierceness of his voice, her eyes went a little wild and unfocused, and he tempered his expression. The last thing she needed after a shock like this was an interrogation from him. "Sorry. Go on."

"I came home just before I called you and...and saw it like this. I don't know what happened."

Another siren cut through the night before he could ask her anything more. His backup pulled in behind him and Chris Hernandez climbed out of the squad car, her eyes wide and astonished.

"Sweet Almighty. What happened here?"

"I don't know," he said grimly. "But I'm sure as hell going to find out."

He was suddenly glad Chris was the responding officer. She was a good cop, one of his best. Beyond that, the fact that she was a woman might help make Sarah a little more at ease.

"Can you stay here in the Bronco with Miss Mc-Kenzie until the ambulance arrives?"

Sarah made a small, distressed sound and grabbed his arm. "I don't need an ambulance. I'm fine."

"Sweetheart, you're more pale than that moon up there."

"Please, Jesse. I feel foolish enough as it is. I don't need an ambulance. Honestly."

After a moment of indecision, he instructed Chris to cancel the ambulance but to stay with Sarah while he looked around. "Call in the county crime scene unit, too," he added. "I'm afraid this is a bigger job than we can handle alone"

"Sure, Chief."

He walked toward the house, noting that neighbors had already been drawn to the sirens like flies to a corpse. With the prurient interest of the uninvolved, they stood on their front porches, craning their necks to see what was happening.

At least they were keeping their distance. Nobody else should have to see this.

Up close, Jesse was even more sickened by the mess. The blood or whatever it was hadn't just been randomly splashed around. Whoever had done this wanted to destroy—the bastard had set out to do the most damage possible. Dark stains covered everything. The trim of the porch, the windowsill, a white wicker planter full of cheerful pink flowers.

Worse, words had been painted on the white of her door. Terrible, vile obscenities—names that shouldn't be used against anyone, especially not a woman like Sarah McKenzie.

He dipped a finger into one of the puddles of red and brought it to his nose. Definitely blood, judging by the metallic tang. Where the hell had so much blood come from? It would have to be an animal, he decided. Or a couple of animals, even. The forensics lab could have that information to him in just a few hours.

Whatever it came from, the blood was still wet, which meant the vandal had finished up probably no longer than twenty minutes ago. What if Sarah had come home and caught him in the act?

His stomach churned at the thought. Anyone capable of this kind of viciousness would be capable of anything.

He suddenly noticed something even more worrisome, something he had overlooked in the shock of seeing all that blood. The blood wasn't the worst of the damage. Every single window he could see had been systematically shattered.

The raw savagery of it shocked him. This hadn't been a random act, but something aimed specifically at her. What could she possibly have done to make someone this angry at her?

A quick look around her house showed that most of the damage was confined to the front where it would have the most shock value. He was just about to head back to the Bronco and wait for the sheriff's crime scene unit when he spotted something on the porch, something he'd missed the first time through.

A men's baseball-type cap with an embroidered logo of an olive nymph dry fly on it was lying in a puddle of blood. The cap was dirty, as all good fishing caps are, but the only blood he could see on it was underneath, where it rested in the puddle, which likely meant it had landed there after the vandal had done his work.

As a clue, it wasn't much. Half the men in town probably owned a similar kind of cap. But maybe forensics could lift prints off it. He used a pen to pick it up, then walked back toward the flashing lights.

Hernandez slipped out of the Bronco to talk to him, closing the door behind her so Sarah couldn't hear their conversation.

"How is she?" he asked the officer.

She shrugged. "Pretty shook up. I keep trying to talk to her, you know, just to make conversation, but she acts like she doesn't even know I'm there. What's her story?"

"She's just a nice lady who doesn't deserve to have something like this happen to her."

"It's more than that. You haven't been sitting there with her, Chief. It's spooky, if you ask me. I've seen it before with crime victims. It's almost like she's not here, like she's gone somewhere else inside her head. Something's definitely weird with her."

"This would be a shock for anyone to come home and find on their doorstep."

"Maybe. And maybe she knows who it is. Maybe that's why she's so scared."

He didn't like the implications of that idea at all, that Sarah had reason to know who might be terrorizing her.

"You find anything up there besides a nasty mess and words that would get my mouth washed out with soap every day for the rest of my life if my mama saw them?" Chris asked.

"Just this." He held up the baseball cap. "I want to see if she recognizes it, then you can bag it and hand it over to CSI. Why don't you start canvasing the neighbors and see if anybody saw or heard anything?"

Inside the Bronco he found Sarah staring through the passenger window with wide, unblinking eyes. He wanted to pull her into his arms, to tuck her head under his chin and hold that trembling body against him until his heat warmed her skin, warmed her soul.

He couldn't do any of those things, though. All he could do was try his best to find the sick animal who had done this.

He held up the baseball cap. "Do you recognize this?"

She blinked several times, as if sliding back into the present. "I…I don't think so. Do you believe it belongs to the person who…" Her voice trailed off as if she couldn't quite find the right words.

It didn't matter. He knew what she meant. "Seems likely. I found it on the porch. It doesn't have any splatters on it, which makes me think it wasn't there when most of the blood was spilled."

She drew a ragged-sounding breath. "So it *is* blood. I thought…I was hoping it might be paint."

"No. Definitely blood. Probably from an animal, maybe a cow or something."

She said nothing for several moments, mulling over the information, then she turned to him again. "How much longer before I can begin cleaning it up? Mr. Jimenez will be angry if it stains."

"Forget Bob. I'll send someone to clean it up in the morning after the crime scene investigators are done."

"I have to do it tonight, Jesse. I won't be able to sleep inside there, knowing all this is out here."

At the tremble in her voice, he again fought the urge to pull her into his arms. "Sweetheart, I don't know if you noticed, but most of your windows are shattered. We can put boards up tonight, but it's going to take time to order replacements for them."

She looked at the house once more and seemed to

crumple. This time he lost the internal battle he was waging and reached for her. She came to him willingly, as if she had been waiting just for this, and settled her head against his chest.

"If you think for one second that I'm letting you stay there alone tonight, you're crazy," Jesse murmured against her hair. "You're coming home with me."

After a moment she pulled away. "I can take care of myself."

She said the words firmly, and he knew she was trying to convince herself as much as him. A soft, aching tenderness settled in his heart.

"I know you can take care of yourself. But you shouldn't have to. Not after this. I'm sorry, but you're going to have to stay with me. I would take you out to the ranch, but with the girls sick, I think Ellie has all she can handle right now."

"I don't want to impose. I could stay at a hotel until the windows are fixed."

"Let me do this, Sarah. Please?"

She looked at the carnage outside her house for a long time, then finally nodded.

Both of them knew she didn't have much choice.

She stood under Jesse Harte's shower for a long time, long after her skin was red and puckered from the heat, long after her aching knee couldn't hold her upright anymore and she had sunk to the tile with her arms wrapped around herself, huddling there and trembling.

But still she couldn't seem to get clean.

He had found her. It was the only explanation she could come up with.

Somehow Tommy DeSilva had escaped from prison and come to find her.

Who else would have reason to hate her so badly? She couldn't think of a soul. Surely no one in Star Valley would do such a thing.

Ever since she had seen what had been done to her house, she had teetered back and forth on the thin line between flashback and reality. She felt as if she had spent the past eighteen months trying to wake up from a horrible nightmare, only to have it sneak up on her again when she least expected it.

Just the thought of being in the same state with Tommy DeSilva sent panic churning through her veins.

When she realized who must have vandalized her house, her first instinct had been to flee, to pack up her car and leave Star Valley behind. But she was afraid if she started running, she would never be able to stop. She would spend the rest of her life looking over her shoulder, always waiting for him to find her.

Still shivering, she wrapped herself in the warm towel Jesse had provided, then reached for the robe he had been thoughtful enough to instruct that kind female officer—Officer Hernandez, wasn't it?—to pack for her, along with a few of her other possessions.

She would have to tell him.

All of it. The awful, sordid details of what had happened in Chicago. He would have to know so that he could start looking for DeSilva.

Dear heavens, she didn't want to tell him. She stared at her reflection in the mirror, a hot, heavy ache welling up in her throat. When she told him, he would never be able to look at her the same way again. He would see the same stranger she saw staring back at her in the mirror right now.

A victim.

As much as she wanted to stay silent, she knew tonight's events had taken that choice out of her hands. She had to tell Jesse everything. He had to know the ugliness she had somehow unleashed on his town, however unwittingly.

She tied her robe tightly and went to find him.

The first creature she met outside the bathroom was the huge golden retriever he had introduced as Daisy. The dog was lying in the hall, chin on her paws, as if waiting for Sarah. Sarah found great comfort in her presence, like having a big shaggy guardian angel.

At the sight of her, the dog wagged her long tail and rose gracefully to her feet, then led the way down the hall.

Jesse was in his kitchen, a surprisingly efficient nook with pine cupboards and wood floors that opened to a larger, carpeted living area. He was barefoot, she saw, and couldn't for the life of her figure out why she found that so appealing.

"How was your shower? Did you have enough hot water?"

There probably wasn't enough hot water in the whole town to keep her warm. "Yes," she lied. "Plenty."

"Good. I was just brewing you some tea. My sister, Cass, swears it's the cure for everything, from hangnails to PMS. Why don't you sit down and I'll bring you a cup?"

She nodded and, with her retriever shadow, walked to the sitting area next to the kitchen.

Even though the night was mild, Jesse had lit a small fire in the stone fireplace, and tears stung her eyes at his thoughtfulness. The warmth washed over, enfolded her like a thick quilt, seeping into her chilled bones as she sat down on a couch covered in fabric of dark blues and greens.

Daisy immediately settled into what looked like her customary spot, atop a braided oval rug in front of the fireplace.

"Here we go." Jesse brought her tea in a mug with a leaping trout on the side. "Can I get you anything else? I can make you a sandwich if you would like."

The thought of food made her stomach churn greasily. "No. I...no. Tea is fine."

He took a seat in the wide recliner that was obviously *his* customary spot and watched until she took a sip of the strong herbal tea. To her surprise, it did make her feel somewhat better. She could feel the panic recede just a little further.

"It's good," she murmured. "Thank you."

They talked for a few moments about innocuous things—the weather, the sports team he liked, his sister, Cassie, who had decorated the house for him when he bought it the year before. He was trying his best to put her at ease, she realized, touched by his efforts.

She was almost tempted to just stay there sipping tea, savoring the hiss and crackle of the fire, blocking out any of the ugliness of the evening or of that morning so many months ago in Chicago.

But she couldn't put it off. She had to tell him.

It was so much harder than she thought it would be. Like the story she read her class of squeezing water from stone.

"Jesse, I have to tell you something," she finally just blurted out.

He frowned at her tone. "What's wrong?"

"I...I lied to you earlier."

His frown deepened. "You what?"

"I lied. I told you I don't know who might have been responsible for vandalizing my house."

"But you do?"

She took a deep, shuddering breath for strength. "His name is Tommy DeSilva. I don't know how it's possible, but I think he must have found me somehow and followed me from Chicago."

"Why would he do that?"

She couldn't look at him. She couldn't watch the pity and revulsion she knew would appear on those strong, masculine features.

She felt a quick, sharp pang of loss, knowing that after she told him, he would definitely never kiss her again as he had the day before on the mountainside.

Not that she expected him to, but this would definitely make such a likelihood impossible.

"Because my testimony sent him to prison for rape and attempted murder," she answered.

He was quiet for a long time and when he finally spoke, his voice sounded strained. "Who was his victim?"

He knows, she thought. She could hear it in his voice, that thin thread of pity and shock already filtering through. But still he needed to hear the words. She needed to *say* the words.

She looked at her tightly laced fingers, at the glossy fabric of her robe, at the oatmeal weave of his carpet.

At anything but him.

"Me," she finally whispered. "Eighteen months ago, Tommy DeSilva attacked me and…and raped me and left me to die."

Chapter 10

At her stark words, Jesse froze, his breath a tight and heavy ache in his chest.

A million emotions surged through him: shock, dismay, sorrow. Most of all, a fierce, overriding fury at the son of a bitch who had hurt her.

He should have guessed her secrets before. A fine cop he was. She had thrown out enough clues to stop a damn train.

Maybe he had suspected it, deep in his subconscious. He'd seen enough crime victims over the years that he must have picked up at least some of the signs.

But maybe he hadn't wanted to see what was right in front of him, to face the grim reality that someone as good and decent as Sarah could suffer such brutality.

So many things about her now made sense. Those dark shadows in her eyes, her skittishness around him and just about every other man he had ever seen her with. That slight, subtle limp.

He started to speak and had to clear the raw choke-hold of emotion from his throat before he could get the words out. "Is your knee injury from the attack?"

Her head barely moved when she nodded.

She watched him out of those serious green eyes and he knew she was waiting for some kind of reaction from him. What the hell was he supposed to say to her after a bombshell like that?

I'm sorry? She had to know he was.

I wish it had never happened to you? The words were a vast understatement.

I'd like to find the bastard who hurt you and rip him apart with my bare hands? He sensed the ragged ferocity of his emotions would only upset her more.

So what was he supposed to say? To do? He wanted to go to her and pull her from the couch and into his arms. He wanted to hold her close and whisper soft kisses into her hair and promise he wouldn't let anybody ever hurt her again.

But he didn't have the right to promise her anything.

"Do you want to know about it?" she asked quietly at his continued silence.

Did he? No. He wanted to pretend it had never happened, that something so ugly had never even touched her. Every instinct in him wanted to urge her to stay quiet.

Somehow he knew that the telling would change both of them.

But he couldn't give in to those strident voices. It *had* happened. She had been brutally attacked. And she had survived. It seemed small and selfish of him to want to pretend it had never happened, just because he wasn't sure *he* could handle hearing about it.

Besides that, he sensed she needed to tell him.

"It might help us in our investigation, if this guy is really in town." He tried to keep his voice even, hoping like hell the jumble of fury and reluctance and heartache he was feeling didn't filter through.

She was quiet for a moment, her hands wound tightly in her lap. The only sound in the house was Daisy's snuffly breathing and the snapping fire on the grate. Then she finally spoke.

"I taught third grade in Chicago," she began. "Eight- and nine-year-olds. It was a poor, inner-city school, in quite a rough area. My parents couldn't understand why I didn't take a job in Evanston closer to Northwestern, where they both are professors, but I loved my job. The children were so eager to learn, just fascinated by everything I taught them." Her soft smile damn near broke his heart.

She paused for several seconds and he sensed she was trying to gather her courage to reach the crux of the story. "I...I had a student named Beatriz DeSilva. I know teachers aren't supposed to have favorites, but I have to confess, she was always one of mine. She had these beautiful long, glossy braids and the sweetest smile."

That soft smile of remembrance teased at her mouth again, but quickly fluttered away. She swallowed hard. "One day out on the playground, I told her to put on her mittens. It was a really awful day, with a bitter wind blowing off the lake. Other than that, it seemed like just a normal day."

Her voice took on a faraway quality. "It seemed as if everything moved in slow motion. Bea reached into her pocket for her mittens, just as I had asked her to do, but when she pulled her hands out, something else fell out as well and landed on the blacktop. A small bundle containing several packets of dirty white powder.''

"Cocaine?"

She shook her head. "Heroin. With a street value of nearly two thousand dollars."

Children in third grade shouldn't even know what heroin looked like, let alone carry it in their pockets along with their mittens. He was disgusted, but not really surprised. Unfortunately, he had seen and heard much worse. "What did you do?"

"Bea was wailing and shaking, terrified out of her wits that I had seen the drugs. I pulled her into the classroom and made her tell me everything. I've never seen a child so frightened." Sarah folded her hands together tightly. "She finally broke down and told me that her older brother Tommy fancied himself a big-time dealer in the area. He was all of eighteen. He sometimes used her to drop small shipments for his clientele, forcing her to do it with threats that he would hurt their baby brother if she didn't."

She cleared her throat before continuing. "Bea was supposed to have delivered the drugs that morning before school, but for some reason she didn't. We were having a special assembly first thing that morning and she didn't want to be late for it. I never would have found out what her brother was putting her through if not for that."

She clamped her lips together and he watched her pulse quiver in her throat. "I was so furious. She was only a child. Just a sweet little girl doing what she was told to protect her baby brother. I immediately called the police. Bea and her little brother were turned over to social services while officers went looking for Tommy."

"They didn't find him?"

"Oh, they did." Her bitter smile held no mirth. "He was arrested and charged, but released on bail six hours later."

"And he came looking for you." A statement, not a question. He knew enough about the criminal mind to know that sometimes vengeance came before anything else. Food, drugs, sex. They all paled in comparison to getting even.

Beneath her robe, her shoulders trembled just a little with her shudder. "He broke a window into my classroom and was waiting for me the next morning when I arrived at school."

His retriever whimpered at the distress in Sarah's voice, then rose from her spot by the fire and padded to her. Jesse was about to order her down, but he stopped, sensing Sarah was drawing a comfort from the dog he wasn't sure he could provide.

Daisy rested her chin on Sarah's knee and she patted her absently, her fingers working through the long yellow fur like worry beads.

"I was there early to catch up with some work," she finally continued. "If I had been a half hour later, the other classrooms in that hall would have been filled with teachers and I could have called for help. But there was no one else there."

"What happened?" The words felt like tiny sharp stones in his raw throat.

"I think he was more upset at losing the drugs than anything else. He kept saying he owed people and now I owed him. Stupid me, I was more angry than scared at first. I told him he was worse than an animal for endangering a child."

She blew out a breath. "I shouldn't have baited him.

That's when he hit me. He—he had a gun and he hit me on the side of the head with it. The impact stunned me and I fell to the floor, and I can remember lying there on that faded, dirty tile, thinking I was going to die. That this punk—this stupid, hopped-up gangbanger—was going to kill me.''

He couldn't even begin to imagine the horror or the courage it must be taking her to tell him about it. ''He didn't fire the gun?''

''No. I'm not sure why. I guess he must have realized that would have brought people running. He used it to hit me, though. He just kept hitting me and hitting me with whatever he could find. The gun, a chair, a stapler, a chair, his fists.''

Stop. Enough. He couldn't stand hearing any more. He growled a harsh oath, intending to beg her to stop this grim recital, but she didn't seem to hear him, lost in the past.

''It seemed like it lasted forever, but it was probably only a few moments. Eventually I stopped fighting and came close to passing out. That's when he...he raped me, then he left. I was terrified he would come back, but after a few minutes I somehow managed to crawl out into the hall and the custodian found me.''

She paused. ''I remember feeling so grateful that at least my students didn't have to see me that way.''

This time her tiny smile did break his heart. He felt it shatter into jagged shards.

''Oh, Sarah. I'm so sorry.'' He couldn't keep silent any longer, whether he said the wrong words or not.

She blinked at him and he watched her click back into the present. Color soaked her cheeks and she became suddenly fascinated with Daisy's fur. ''DeSilva must be in Star Valley. He's the only one I know who…who hates me enough to do something like that to my home.''

"Can you describe him so I can tell my officers what they might be looking for?"

She closed her eyes as if picturing him in her mind, and he was struck again by her delicate features, by soft skin stretching over the hollows and curves of her face. He wanted to skim his fingers over that face, to trace the dark smudge of her lashes and the thin bridge of her nose.

How could a woman who seemed so vulnerable have survived such an ordeal? Maybe that was the reason for her fragility, because she *had* survived and was still trying to find her way in the aftermath.

"He was big for eighteen," she said. "Probably your height, muscled like a body builder. He had a small beard back then, just a little fuzz on his chin. I remember thinking he barely seemed old enough for facial hair. He might have shaved it off by now."

He hated making her relive any more details, but the more information his officers had, the better the chances of finding the bastard if he was indeed in Star Valley. He almost hoped DeSilva was dumb enough to come after her. If he was here, Jesse would find him.

"Any other defining characteristics? A tattoo or anything?"

"Nothing very original. He had a snake twining around his arm and a four-lettered obscenity tattooed across his knuckles."

"That will help. That kind of thing is pretty rare around here." He rose, grateful to be able to take some action, no matter how small. "I'll call this description in to my officers and the sheriff's department and also get someone on the phone to Chicago so they can fax us a mug. Are you okay here for a few moments while I do that?''

She nodded, and watched him cross the room toward the phone with quick, restless movements. He was like a dark storm cloud, simmering with barely contained energy.

What was he thinking? She wished she could read his emotions better. She knew he was upset. By the time she'd finished giving him the ugly details, he had been barely breathing, as motionless—and dangerous—as a rattlesnake poised to strike. But she couldn't read much more into his features than that.

Everything would be different now. He knew the truth and they could never go back to the casual, friendly place they had been before.

She could hear him on the phone describing Tommy DeSilva to his officers, a hardness to his voice she seldom heard. She found it oddly comforting.

Jesse would keep her safe.

No matter what wild creatures clawed at her subconscious, he would hold them at bay.

Daisy settled a little deeper into sleep, her weight heavy on Sarah's bare feet like one huge furry slipper. Despite the tumult of her emotions, she had to smile. Apparently Jesse wasn't her only self-appointed protector. Anyone who wanted to get to her would have to make it past not just one very large and dangerous man but his ferociously amiable golden retriever, as well.

Jesse ended the call a few moments later and returned to the sitting area. ''I put out the word that we're looking for any suspicious strangers in town. It's a little too early in the season for many tourists to be passing through on their way to Jackson Hole or Yellowstone, so if this DeSilva is anywhere around, he'll stand out like a Christmas tree in July."

"Thank you."

He shrugged. "For what? I'm just doing my job."

"For that and for letting me stay here. I'll try to get out of your hair as soon as I can."

He narrowed his gaze. "You're not going anywhere until we catch whoever did a number on your house tonight, so you might as well just accept it."

Her spine stiffened, vertebra by vertebra. She appreciated his protectiveness—it warmed a small, cold place inside her. But she had been a victim long enough.

She refused to completely surrender her life.

If DeSilva wanted her badly enough, she knew he would find her, whether here or at her own place.

"I'll stay until I can get someone to clean up the mess and replace the windows. When the house is ready again, I'll move back."

He opened his mouth as if he were gearing up for a fierce argument, then closed it again. "If we're no further along in the investigation by that time, we can talk about it."

"All right." She was suddenly exhausted. So tired she could hardly move, and her knee throbbed viciously.

Jesse picked up on it instantly. "Why don't you get some rest? You can sleep in tomorrow. I can have Cassie come over, if you'd like."

"No. I have school."

"Seems to me you have a good excuse to find a substitute and take the day off."

Chuck Hendricks would just love that. "No. I need to be there. We're having a test in math later."

He sighed at her stubbornness. ''Come on, then. I'll show you to the guest room.''

Sarah tried to stand, but having seventy-five pounds of dog sleeping on her feet made it a challenge.

''What's wrong?'' Jesse asked when she didn't follow him down the hall, then he realized her predicament. ''Sorry. Daisy. Come,'' he ordered. His retriever creaked sadly to her feet but spoiled the effect by bounding over to him like a puppy.

He led the way down the hall and opened a door across from the bathroom where she had showered. He held the door open for her, wide enough for three of her to pass him without even brushing against his shirt.

She noticed the careful distance he maintained between them—as if he were afraid to touch her—and her heart wept a little.

''Are you sure you'll be all right?''

She nodded, not trusting her voice. Everything was different, just as she knew it would be. What would he say if she could somehow find the words to tell him how badly she needed the warmth and safety of his arms around her just then?

She couldn't ask. She wasn't sure she could bear it if he held her with stiff awkwardness, like some fragile piece of glass.

''Good night,'' she finally said, then closed the door between them.

The guest room was large with an inviting, queen-size pine bed covered with a log-cabin quilt in rich plums and greens. A small lamp graced a matching table next the bed and she fought the urge to turn it on. She wasn't afraid of the dark. She wouldn't allow herself to be. The thin spear of moonlight shining through the window would have to be enough.

She climbed into bed and pulled the quilt to her chin,
focusing on that ribbon of light, on the soft texture of
the cotton sheets, on the low murmur of his voice on
the telephone, probably checking on the investigation.
The smell of him lingered in the room—laundry soap
mingled with the woodsy cedar scent of his aftershave.

The exhaustion was still there weighing down her
muscles, but she knew sleep would be a long time coming. Despite her weariness, her body still seethed with
tension, her mind still raced.

She supposed she would have found it shocking if
she *had* been able to drift off easily after the stress of
the evening. Not when she had just been forced to relive in graphic detail the nightmare she had been desperately trying to forget for the past eighteen months.

She thought of the shock on Jesse's hard, beautiful
features as she had told him. That subtle withdrawal
she knew he probably wasn't even aware of. She had
seen it, though. The distance still hurt, even though she
had been expecting nothing less.

She had seen variations on the same theme with
everyone in Chicago after her attack.

Her friends hadn't known what to say. They wanted
to pretend it had never happened, wanted her to just
get over it and go back to the old Sarah.

Her parents had been devastated. Her mother had
wept for days, her father had retreated into his study.
They had insisted she come to their quiet home after
the two weeks she spent in the hospital, and had babied
her as if she were four years old again.

Underlying their reaction had been subtle, unspoken
accusation. If she hadn't stubbornly insisted on teaching at an inner-city school, if she'd been in Evanston,
where she belonged, it never would have happened.

And there was Andrew. The man she had been prepared to spend the rest of her life with. She should have been able to turn to him for comfort after the attack, but she hadn't even been able to face him when he came to the hospital.

She knew she was more to blame for the collapse of their relationship after the rape than he was. She also knew it couldn't have been very solid to begin with if it couldn't survive this test. That didn't stop the harsh sting of failure.

It felt strange to speak of her attack. She hadn't told anyone but Jesse in the nine months since she'd come to Salt River. Not a word. If she didn't speak of it, she could try her best to pretend it never happened to her— that it was some other poor woman who had endured those terrible moments in that dingy, tired classroom.

Besides, it wasn't exactly the sort of thing she could bring up in casual conversation with the other teachers. *May I use the copy machine after you? Oh, by the way, did I mention I was brutally beaten and raped at my previous school?*

She sighed and rolled to her side, toward the window and that pale, comforting slice of moon.

She could still hear Jesse moving around in the other part of the house and she was suddenly struck by the realization that this was the first night she had spent in the same house with another person since she had moved out of her parents' big house and come to Salt River.

So why did she feel more alone than ever?

She absolutely did not want to go back in there.

Friday afternoon, Sarah sat in her car trying to find

enough strength somewhere deep inside her that would carry her up those steps and into Jesse's house.

She wasn't sure she could survive this another night. For five days she had smiled and made small talk and tried to pretend she was comfortable living in his house, that she didn't notice the tension simmering between them.

The effort was exhausting her.

One more night. That's all she had to get through. The company making the custom windows for her rental had promised they would send workmen to install them in the morning, even though it was Saturday.

She just had to get through another evening trying to pretend her feelings for Jesse weren't growing stronger with every passing moment.

He wouldn't be home for another hour or two. In the few days she had been staying there, they had fallen into a routine of sorts—awkward though it was.

She would stop at the grocery store on the way to his house after school and start dinner, then play out in the yard with Daisy for a while.

When his shift ended, Jesse would come home and they would discuss their respective days while they shared a meal. She told him of her students and school politics and her inevitable end-of-the-school-year blues. He would talk about his officers and the calls he'd gone on that day and his inevitable pain-in-the-neck paperwork.

After dinner he would wash up, then stretch out in his favorite chair with the newspaper or a book or the remote while she sat at his kitchen table grading papers. A few torturous hours later, she would eventually give up this test of endurance and retire to the guest room for another sleepless night.

She knew entirely too many things about Jesse Harte after sharing such close quarters with him for nearly a week.

She knew he woke early to run or lift weights, and that when he worked up a sweat, his hair clung to his neck in thick dark spikes.

She knew he laughed at silly jokes his nieces told him over the phone, and that the sound of it—rich and full and generous—could work itself down her spine and leave her breathless.

She knew he was passionate about his job, and considered any crime that took place in his town a personal affront.

And she knew she was teetering precariously close to falling in love with him.

That was why she sat in her car like the craven coward that she was, trying to summon the courage to make it through one more night. Each moment she spent with him, she slipped a little further down that dangerous slope, and it scared her senseless.

It was completely ridiculous, she knew that. Pathetic, even. The shy, skittish schoolteacher pining over the most gorgeous man in town. It was even more pathetic when the man in question couldn't bring himself to touch her in even the most casual of ways.

She sighed. And there was the truth of the matter. That's why she dreaded going inside—because every night, she came closer and closer to begging him to touch her again, to kiss her as he had the day they went riding together.

Only one more night. She could be strong for one more night, couldn't she? She would go home in the morning, whether the dratted windows were installed or not. Heaven knew, she dreaded making a fool of herself over him far more than she feared going back to her house.

A rap on her car window suddenly startled her out of her thoughts. Her heart jumped until she recognized Jesse's younger sister standing outside her car, her short dark hair ruffled in the breeze and her blue eyes clouded with worry.

"Is everything okay?" Cassie Harte asked, her voice muffled by the layer of glass.

Sarah nodded, aware of the heat soaking her cheeks. She must look like an idiot, sitting out here in her car staring at his house. She opened the door and climbed out. "Everything's fine. I was just unwinding for a moment before I went inside."

"I'm sorry to disturb you, then."

Sarah laughed ruefully. "I'm glad you did. Daisy's probably going crazy wondering why I'm just sitting out here."

A pang of discomfort settled in her stomach as she used the key Jesse had given her to unlock his door. She knew she was probably being silly, but it seemed so presumptuous to act as if she belonged here in the house of this woman's brother.

She knew Cassie, but only casually. Early in the school year she had seen quite a bit of her at school functions with Lucy, and had heard from one of the other mothers that Cassie had basically raised her niece until Matt Harte married Ellie Webster over a month before.

She wasn't sure what had happened to Lucy's mother, but by a few of the whisperings she'd heard, apparently she'd disappeared in the midst of some kind of horrible scandal involving Cassie's ex-fiancé.

Sarah also knew Cassie had moved away from the

family ranch after her brother's wedding and now had a job cooking at the Lost Creek dude ranch north of town.

She didn't know much about her, but she did know she liked Cassie. From the time she first moved to Star Valley, the other woman had gone out of her way to make Sarah feel welcome.

Cassie followed her up the stairs and into the house, loaded with boxes and bags. "Nobody in this family tells me anything," she said. "I swear, I would probably still believe in Santa Claus if I had to rely on my big brothers to fill me in. I didn't have a clue what had happened to your house or that you were staying here, until this morning when I ran into Ellie at the grocery store. How are you doing?"

"Fine. Anxious for things to get back to normal, but fine."

"I can understand that. I love him dearly, but I'll be the first to admit Jesse's not always the easiest person to live with. I also know he's not much of a cook— believe me, I know—so I brought a few ready-to-heat dinners. That's why I dropped by. I hope you don't mind."

Ah. So that explained the mystery of her packages. "That's very sweet of you, but I'm going home tomorrow."

Cassie's shrug looked elegantly feminine, despite her T-shirt. "You can take some food back to your house with you or Jesse can always freeze them for another time."

Cassie set a box down on the counter between the kitchen and family room and began removing foil-covered containers. "Hope you like spicy food. Since

I wasn't sure of your tastes, I went by Jesse's. The hotter the better for him.''

She thought of the Thai food she used to devour by the cartonful in Chicago. She hadn't realized she missed it until right this second. ''Spicy is fine.''

''Good. This one is plain old lasagna and this one is artichoke heart enchiladas. Two of his favorites. I've written cooking instructions on each one, but basically you just have to throw them in the oven. Oh, and here's a couple of salads and some bread sticks and turtle pie for dessert.''

Sarah laughed helplessly. ''Whoa. Slow down. This is more food than I could eat in a week.''

''If you were alone, maybe, but if I know my brother, you'll be lucky to get seconds of any of it. Now, which one would you like tonight, lasagna or enchiladas? Just choose and I'll get it started for you.''

''Um, which would you say is your brother's favorite?''

''That's a tough one. He loves them both, but I'd probably have to say the lasagna would squeak ahead, just barely.''

''Lasagna it is, then.''

Cassie turned on the oven, then began working in the kitchen with quick, efficient movements that made Sarah feel like a complete incompetent.

''You know, you really don't have to do this,'' she said. ''I can probably follow directions.''

Cassie's smile lit up her whole pixie face. ''I know. But cooking is what I do best, so don't spoil it for me.''

While Cassie put the foil tray in the oven and began to transfer the rest of the food to the refrigerator, Sarah went to work preparing the salad.

''So tell me,'' Cassie said while they worked, ''is

Jesse any closer to finding out who vandalized your place?''

Sarah shook her head. "He had a couple of leads, but neither one amounted to much."

If anything, he and his officers were further than ever from finding who had made such a mess at her house. Jesse had learned the vandal had used cow's blood—apparently from a cow that was killed and mutilated in a pasture near the Diamond Harte.

Monday morning he had also called Chicago and learned Tommy DeSilva was still in a maximum-security facility in Joliet. DeSilva might have sent someone after her, but Jesse didn't seem to think it was very likely. It seemed an unusually long time to wait for revenge, when he could have more easily sent someone after her when she was still in Evanston staying with her parents.

Which left the terrifying conclusion that she had an unknown enemy somewhere in Star Valley. She couldn't even begin to figure out who it might be.

"Well, I hope he finds him fast," Cassie said fiercely. "It makes me sick that someone could terrorize you that way. And I can promise you that when Jesse does find whoever it is, he's going to make the creep very, very sorry. One time in school when I was about seven, he found out that Kip Burton used to tie my shoelaces together every day on the school bus so I'd fall on my face. Kip was a year older than Jesse and twice as big, but that didn't stop my brother."

"What did he do?" Sarah knew she shouldn't be so intrigued by the image of Jesse as a boy.

"He tied Kip's shoelaces together with Wally Martin's, who was even bigger and meaner than Kip. Wally wasn't happy about it, I can tell you that. By the time

Wally was through with him, Kip could barely even tie his own shoes. I think he still holds a grudge to this day."

Sarah's laugh was the first genuine one she had enjoyed in a week. When the sound of it faded, the kitchen fell silent except for Daisy slurping at her water bowl. She glanced at Cassie and found the other woman watching her closely, a strange light in her eyes.

"I think you're really wonderful for Jesse," his sister said quietly.

Sarah flushed. "Oh, no. We don't...I mean, we're not... You've got it all wrong."

Cassie didn't look convinced. "That's too bad. He needs someone like you in his life."

"What do you mean?"

Cassie was silent for a long moment, and Sarah felt her scrutiny and wondered at it. After a moment, she spoke.

"Our parents were killed in a car accident when Jesse was seventeen. Did you know that?"

She had wondered about the elder Hartes, but no one had ever told her their fate and she'd never dared ask. "I'm sorry," she said softly. "That must have been horrible for all of you. How old were you?"

"I was twelve. Matt was twenty-one. It *was* hard on Matt and me, but I think their deaths hit Jesse the hardest. He was the only one in the truck with them when Dad hit a patch of ice in the canyon between here and Jackson. The truck rolled about a hundred feet down a steep embankment and almost into the Snake River."

Sarah made a soft sound of distress and wondered why Cassie was telling her this.

"Mom and Dad weren't wearing seat belts," she

went on, "and they had massive injuries. I think Jesse knew they were dying, but that didn't stop him from going for help."

Sorrow for what he must have gone through squeezed her insides. "Was he injured?"

Cassie nodded, a faraway look in those startling blue eyes so much like her brothers'. "His leg was broken in a couple places, his wrist was shattered and his shoulder was dislocated. I can't imagine the kind of pain he must have been in, but he still managed to claw his way through snow and ice, up that steep hill toward the highway. It took him more than an hour. By the time he made it to the top and flagged down help, Mom and Dad were gone."

The kitchen fell silent again as Sarah tried to come up with an adequate response that didn't exist. Before she could say anything, Cassie continued.

"An experience like that changes a person. Jesse was always a little wild, but after Mom and Dad died, he spiraled out of control. Drinking, partying, fighting with anybody who even looked at him wrong. Matt must have bailed him out of jail a dozen times."

"He must have been hurting so badly." She wanted to cry just thinking about it.

She wasn't sure what she'd said that made Cassie smile so unexpectedly or look at her with that funny light in her eyes again.

"Even worse than the fighting were the women. I swear, he dated every bimbo between here and Cheyenne. It's about time he realized he deserves better than that. He deserves a woman like you. Someone warm and smart and decent."

If Cassie only knew how far off the mark she was!

The last thing Jesse needed in his life was a woman with the kind of problems Sarah had.

"Well, as I said, you have the wrong idea about us. I'm only staying here because Jesse wouldn't let me check in to a hotel and I didn't know where else to go. Your brother and I are only friends."

They were, she realized with surprise. She genuinely liked and respected him. She had told him things no one else in Star Valley knew about and she trusted completely that he would keep her secrets.

"Well, you can't blame a sister for hoping."

The door opened before Sarah could come up with a suitable reply. An instant later, the subject of their conversation loomed in the doorway, looking big and dark and gorgeous in his uniform.

Cassidy chuckled—at what, Sarah wasn't exactly sure, but she suspected it had something to do with the sudden blush scorching her cheeks.

"Hey, brat," he greeted his sister, but there was clear affection in his expression and in his voice. "I thought you were too busy with those fancy rich cowboy wannabes you're cooking for now at the Lost Creek to bother hanging around us lesser mortals. What are you doing here?"

She sniffed. "I brought food. But if you're going to make fun of my new gig, maybe I'll just take my lasagna and leave."

His face brightened like a kid waiting outside the gates of Disneyland for the park to open for the day. "You brought lasagna? And bread sticks, too? Sarah, sweetheart, did I ever tell you my baby sister is a goddess in the kitchen?"

Sarah swallowed hard at that devastating grin.

"It should be ready as soon as the timer goes off."

Cassie gathered up the boxes she had carried the food in. "Since you already tossed the salad, all you need to do is heat the bread sticks in the microwave for just a few seconds."

"You're leaving?"

"You know me. Always on the run."

"Why don't you stay and eat dinner with us?" Sarah asked. It was such a brilliant idea she was amazed she hadn't thought of it earlier. Cassie could provide a much-needed buffer between her and Jesse and maybe ease some of the tension that always churned between them.

"Another time. I've got things to do. Sarah, I enjoyed talking with you. It was very educational."

Cassie kissed her brother's cheek, then surprised Sarah by pulling her into an embrace and kissing her cheek.

As she watched her walk out the door, Sarah experienced a brief, fierce moment of regret that there really wasn't anything more between her and Jesse. Not only because of her growing feelings for him, but because she had always wanted a sister. She suddenly knew without question that Cassie Harte would have been perfect.

Jesse leaned his hip on the countertop, enjoying the sight of Sarah busying herself in the kitchen. He loved watching her. She always looked so pretty and flustered, and she blushed whenever she caught him at it.

"You have a nice visit with Cassidy Jane?"

She looked up, a startled look in her eyes. Just as he'd hoped, that appealing color crept over her cheeks. "I had no idea Cassie was short for Cassidy."

He snagged an olive out of the salad and popped it

in his mouth. "Yep. Just like Butch Cassidy. We're all named for outlaws."

"I knew you were. Jesse James, right?"

He smiled his best bandito smile. "Exactly."

"I get the Cassidy and the Jesse James but what about Matt? I admit, I'm not the world's best Wild West historian, but I'm not familiar with any outlaws named Matt."

"Matt's the one who started it all. My dad was the great-grandson of Matt Warner, who rode with Butch and Sundance in the Wild Bunch. Dad was fascinated with stories of the old West that had been handed down in his family and he wanted to name his firstborn after his ancestor. The rest of us just followed the theme."

"Your mother must have been a very understanding woman."

He smiled. "She used to call us her own little wild bunch. Living out on the ranch away from most neighbors, we had to learn to entertain ourselves. We used to play hide and seek, and Mom would pretend she was the sheriff rounding us all up to take us to the lockup. We even made this star out of glitter and construction paper that said Sheriff Mom, and she always kept it on the fridge. She'd pin it on and come looking for us."

He hadn't thought about that star in years. What had happened to the silly thing? It had probably disintegrated years ago. The memory made him smile and a little sad at the same time.

His folks had been gone a long time—sixteen years this winter—but sometimes he still missed them so much, he felt it fill his lungs until he couldn't breathe around it. The grief and the guilt always hit him at the same time.

He looked up and found Sarah watching him out of soft, sorrowful green eyes that saw too damn much.

"Cassie told me about the accident," she said quietly. "I'm so sorry. They sound like they were wonderful people. They would have to be in order to produce such fine children."

"I wish they had lived long enough to see that I'm the one chasing the bad guys now."

"I'm sure they would both be very proud of you," she said, and her soft smile was like a shot of pure mountain air, chasing away the thickness in his lungs.

"You remind me a lot of my mom. She was a teacher, too. Taught seventh-grade English."

"I'm sure that must have put quite a crimp in your junior high school social life, to have your mother always watching over your shoulder."

He laughed. "I don't remember it being too much of a detriment. Somehow I always found a way to keep the worst of my rabble-rousing out of her line of sight."

Sarah looked doubtful. "She probably knew much more than you're giving her credit for. Mothers—and teachers—usually know exactly what you're up to."

"I really hope not," he said vehemently.

Her low laugh slid right to his gut. "I know. I know. You were the bad boy of Salt River, Wyoming, right?"

"You don't believe the hype?"

She shrugged, a rare, teasing light in her eyes that sent need uncoiling inside him like barbed wire. "Sorry, Jesse, but all I've seen is the reformed version."

Now, there was a challenge if he'd ever heard one. "There's still a little bad boy left in me, I can promise you that,'' he murmured, and stepped a little closer to her.

Wariness flickered in her gaze—and something else that he couldn't quite recognize—but she didn't retreat. Not even when he took another step forward and another, then leaned in to back up his words with action.

Chapter 11

He knew he shouldn't be doing this. He could come up with a dozen reasons not to kiss Sarah McKenzie. Hell, a hundred, if he really put his mind to it.

All those excuses might be fine in the abstract, but none of them meant a damn thing in reality. Not when she smelled like a summer garden after a rain shower and when she lifted her face for his kiss with the same trusting beauty of one of those rain-soaked flowers turning toward the sun.

And when his subconscious had spent the past week torturing him with fantasies of doing exactly this.

Just a quick kiss, he vowed to himself, just to taste the sweetness there, to tease her a little, then he would back away and return to his side of the friendly, casual distance they had worked so hard this week to maintain between them.

At the first touch of her mouth under his, silken and warm and welcoming, he forgot about keeping that frustratingly safe chasm between them. Forgot about treating her with polite, casual restraint.

All he could focus on was the slick heat of her mouth against his and the way her slender body bowed so perfectly in his arms and the way she kissed him back with an enthusiasm that would have startled him if he'd been capable of rational thought.

He wasn't consciously aware of undoing the clip that restrained all that luxurious hair, but somebody did it. He figured it must have been him, since he was the one whose fingers tangled in it, raked through the long, silky strands, tugged it gently so her head fell back to give him better access to her incredible mouth.

She moaned against his mouth. At the sound of it, low and aroused, he lost the last tenuous hold on his control. He deepened the kiss, molding her body to him, letting her feel the strength of his arousal.

Her arms slid around his neck and the movement pressed her small, firm breasts against the muscles of his chest.

Heat rushed to his groin and he pressed one thigh between hers. She wore a skirt and another of those short-sleeved sweater sets, demure and sweet, that somehow still always managed to conjure up all manner of wicked thoughts in his head. This one was pale lavender, and he had no trouble slipping a hand underneath it to caress the achingly soft skin at her waist.

She rewarded him with another of those sexy noises she made, so he pressed his advantage and ventured higher along that expanse of skin, toward the lace covering her breasts. When he was nearly there, she gasped his name, and a small, delicate shudder racked her frame.

He froze, breathing harder than a rookie on his first call, his hand still under her sweater.

What the *hell* was he doing?

He was about to feel up Sarah McKenzie like some kind of randy teenager hoping to get lucky in the back seat of his dad's sedan—even knowing what he did about her past and the scars that had been carved in her soul.

She must be scared to death to have him mauling her like this, after what she'd been through.

Self-disgust roiled through him, sick and hot and greasy. She had trusted him and this is how he repaid her?

It made him feel even worse to realize that even now—when he was fully aware of the gross inappropriateness of groping her while she was a guest in his home—part of him didn't want to stop.

Somehow he mustered strength enough to edge away, though his body groaned in protest.

He shoved his hands into his back pockets. "That was unforgivable, Sarah. I'm so sorry."

Her breathing was as ragged and shallow as his, her eyes dark with confusion. "You're sorry for what?"

"I shouldn't have kissed you. Touched you. I was way out of line."

"No, you weren't. I wanted you to kiss me." She cleared her throat. "And to, um, to touch me."

Her voice was strong and determined even though color coated her cheeks like autumn brushed on leaves. Still, her words did nothing to ease the guilt writhing around inside him.

He raked a hand through his hair. "I promised you would be safe here, and you are. Even from me. *Especially* from me."

"I wanted you to kiss me, Jesse," she repeated. "I've been wanting you to kiss me again since that day on the mountain."

He stared, hearing the exasperation in her voice. "You have?"

"Why do you sound so surprised? If I took a poll, I imagine I'd find that half the women in town probably want you to kiss them."

This time he was amazed to find that *he* was the one blushing. "That's ridiculous," he mumbled.

"It is not. Half the women in town and probably a vastly higher percentage of the women who hang out at the Renegade would stand in line for a chance to be right here."

"That's different. *You're* different."

"Why? I'm still a woman."

Same equipment, maybe, but he could come up with very few other similarities between her and the kind of wild party girls who hung out at the local honky-tonk. "Trust me. You're different. I should never have kissed you."

She was quiet for a moment, then lifted her chin. "Because of what Tommy DeSilva did to me?"

He couldn't lie to her. "That's part of it."

At his words, the color faded from her face and her features seemed as frozen as a mountain lake in January. "I see," she murmured.

But he could tell she didn't. How could she possibly understand, when he wasn't sure he did? She probably was thinking some nonsense about how he didn't find her desirable or that he couldn't get past the fact that she had been raped.

That was so far from the truth, he wanted to laugh. Every moment she spent living in the same house with him, breathing the same air, he only wanted her more. From the moment he walked in the door after work until he somehow made it through the torturous hours until he left again in the morning, he had to fight like hell to keep from touching her, from kissing her, from doing exactly what he'd just done.

She didn't have a clue.

He had worked hard to make sure of it, to conceal as best he could the effect she had on him. The hunger eating away at him. If she'd caught even a glimmer of it, he had no doubts she would have moved back into her shell of a house in a second, broken windows or not.

How would she react if she knew he spent every damn night tossing and turning in his bed, listening for her down the hall, cursing the fact that she was so tantalizingly close but completely out of his reach?

He wanted her with a fierceness that stunned him, but he knew he couldn't act on it. She needed tenderness, gentleness—a delicate, careful touch. How the hell was he supposed to provide those things when he lost control with just a simple kiss?

The plain truth was that he didn't trust himself. He wasn't sure he could give her all those things he knew she needed after what that bastard had done to her.

Yeah, part of the reason he had stopped had to do with Tommy DeSilva. Whenever he thought about her attack, a hot, savage spear of rage lodged in his chest. He had never experienced such mindless fury in his life.

And even though he hadn't known her at the time— even though her attack had happened a thousand miles away—he couldn't shake this strange sense of responsibility, as if the system of justice he believed in so strongly and worked so fiercely to uphold had failed her.

He was a cop, and a damn good one. He should be used to seeing the darker side of society. He was, even in a small town like Salt River. But somehow knowing that a sweet, innocent woman like Sarah had been the victim of something so terrible hit him in the gut like a cannonball whenever he thought about it.

He ached to make everything better for her. It was impossible, he knew that. He couldn't change what had happened to her—hell, he couldn't even find the words to tell her how very sorry he was—and the knowledge made him helpless with frustration.

The timer on the oven went off before he could look for those elusive words once more.

"That's your lasagna." Avoiding both his touch and his gaze, Sarah crossed to the oven and removed the casserole dish with oven mitts. "Shall we eat here at the bar or in the dining room?"

He didn't want to eat. Cassie's lasagna appealed to him about as much as gnawing on cement right about now. Not when the air between them still hummed and sparked with tension.

"Sarah —" he began, but she cut him off.

"Let's eat in the dining room, shall we?"

Her abrupt tone and her cool body language told him she wanted the subject dropped.

He huffed out a breath. As much as he needed to clear the air between them, he refused to force a heated discussion that she would obviously prefer not to have.

Frustration churning through him, he jerked his chair out and sat down.

They went through the motions of eating in silence for several minutes. Finally, just around the time he was ready to climb the walls, she rose from the table. "You know, I'm really not hungry after all. I have a PTA meeting at seven, so I think I'll just run over to the school a little early and try to finish some work in my classroom."

He slid his chair back, noting with a frown that she had barely picked at her food. "I'll go with you."

"That's not necessary."

"I don't want you going out at night by yourself. Not when we still haven't caught the vandal who redecorated your house."

That stubborn chin tilted in the air once more. "It's not necessary," she repeated.

"It is to me."

"Look, Jesse, it's bad enough for my reputation that I have been staying here alone with you all week. If you insist on following me all over town, people might start to get the wrong idea about us. And neither of us would want that, would we?"

Let them get the wrong idea. Maybe then she'd let him past this cool reserve. "Do you really think anybody cares where you're staying?"

"This is a small town with conservative values. I'm a single woman teaching impressionable children. Like it or not, I'm under a microscope. If enough parents complained to Chuck Hendricks about me staying with you, he wouldn't hesitate to fire me."

"I won't go in, then. I'll just drive over behind you to make sure you arrive safely, then I'll come back in a few hours when the meeting's over to see you home."

She opened her mouth to argue, but he cut her off with a glare, all his frustration simmering back. If she wanted him to shut up, he would, but he wasn't going to back down about this. Not when her safety was concerned. ''Damn it, Sarah, I care about you. I don't want anything to happen to you. Just let me do this, all right?''

She blinked at his vehemence, then shrugged. ''Fine. I'll be ready in a few moments.''

She should be paying attention.

Sarah stretched her knee out, wiggled around on her folding metal chair in a vain effort to find a more comfortable position, and tried to focus on the twangy voice of Nancy Larsen.

The PTA president was saying something about next year's fund-raising projects, but she might as well have been speaking pig Latin. Sarah couldn't seem to focus on anything but a certain frustrating, sexy, aggravating police chief.

She had replayed that scene in his kitchen at least a dozen times in the hour since the PTA meeting started. Every touch, every texture, every scent was imprinted on her mind, burned into it like the mark on Corey Sylvester's skin.

Just remembering his mouth on hers—the heat of his body pressed against hers, his hard, callused hands on her skin—turned her insides hollow and weak, her breasts achy and full.

She had wanted the kiss to go on forever. Hours, days, weeks. Forget food, forget sleep, forget anything but Jesse and his incredible mouth and clever, clever hands.

While she was being honest with herself, she might as well admit that she wanted much more than stolen kisses in his kitchen. She wanted to explore the hard muscles of his chest she could see bunch and play under his shirts. She wanted to glide her hands and her mouth over his skin.

She wanted to feel his hard strength inside her.

She shifted on her cold metal chair as color washed over her cheeks. She shouldn't be thinking about this in the middle of a PTA meeting, for heaven's sake!

She couldn't help it, though. It still seemed like some kind of wondrous miracle that she could want him that way, after eighteen months of believing she would never be able to feel the hot pull of desire again.

Unfortunately, what she wanted wasn't important. The reawakening of these long-dormant needs and desires inside her didn't matter. Not when Jesse admitted he couldn't get past what had happened in Chicago.

Telling him had changed everything, just as she had known it would. Just as it had with Andrew.

Like Andrew, Jesse couldn't look at her without remembering what had been done to her. She had seen it in his eyes. He was afraid to touch her, fearful that he would put his hands in the wrong place or say the wrong thing.

That he couldn't be gentle enough.

The hollow yearning in her stomach changed to something else. Something wistful and sorrowful and angry at the same time.

It was always there on the edge of her consciousness, that terrible October morning. Always lurking like some huge, hideous, wild creature, just waiting for her guard to slip so it could stick its vicious claws into her once more.

Since she had come here, she had tried to cope by not telling anyone. If people didn't know, then her attack didn't exist. It wasn't real. It couldn't *possibly* be real.

But Jesse knew now. She had been forced to tell him and now he couldn't touch her without also touching the rabid creature that followed her everywhere.

The young, frizzy-haired rape counselor who had visited her in the hospital right after the attack had given her a thick packet of information. Booklets and hotline numbers and support group schedules, to try to help her process what had happened.

During those long days in the hospital she had forced herself to at least skim through the information, but she hadn't been able to absorb much from it. No one could possibly understand what she was going through, so what was the point in reading about other people's experiences?

Actually, she found it surprising that she remembered anything from that time.

She had been barely there, aware on one level of all the specialists and nurses and therapists checking this monitor and adjusting that medication, coming and going endlessly.

They existed on the periphery, though.

Mostly, she had been cushioned in some merciful limbo, wrapped in a protective cocoon of lethargy where no one could reach her. Where no one could hurt her.

One of the few things she remembered from that barrage of information was one article where the author, herself a victim, had eloquently discussed the culture of isolating silence surrounding women who had been raped.

No one wants to talk about or to hear about it. The crime itself is often considered so unspeakable, so shameful, that its victims are rendered mute, she remembered reading. Their names are omitted from newspaper articles as if they no longer exist, their faces become a blurred, vacant circle on the television.

The loved ones of rape victims especially don't want to talk about it, uncomfortable with the complex ferocity of their own emotions and ravaged by the victim's.

She had seen that in her family and friends. Her mother's tears. Her father's devastated rage. The shock and pity of her friends—and the guilty relief that it had happened to her instead of to them.

And so she had slipped willingly into that silence everyone seemed to expect of her.

She hadn't minded. Not really. She had wanted it that way. Needed it that way. The last thing she wanted to do was rehash the morning that had changed her life, to relive every detail of the attack whenever she looked into the faces of everyone around her.

But now Jesse knew, and he wouldn't touch her because of it.

Sometimes the injustice of it made her want to scream and weep at the same time. She had done nothing to deserve what had happened to her, yet she was still being punished.

Most of all, she hated that her rape hadn't ended when Tommy DeSilva climbed back through that jagged glass of her classroom window. It was not a static, isolated moment, but sometimes seemed to go on and on and on, sucking any color and joy from her life.

She closed her eyes, suddenly exhausted.

She couldn't bear the idea of going back to Jesse's house, to the thick, constant tension between them. She wanted her own space, her soothing, peaceful gardens, the scent of her own pillow.

One more night. She could make it through a few more hours at his house.

And then she would wrap herself once more in her safe, protective, suffocating cloak of silence.

Jesse looked at the clock on the wall of his office, hanging above a framed print of a moose hip-deep in the Snake River, moss dripping from his antlers.

The kid wasn't going to show.

Corey was nearly an hour late for their last run-through of the anticrime presentation they were scheduled to give the next week.

It shouldn't surprise him, since the day seemed to be rapidly changing from bad to worse, starting first thing when he had walked out of his bedroom before his shift that morning to find Sarah headed for the front door, her bags in tow.

He had talked until his teeth ached, trying to convince her to stay at his house a few more days, but she had been adamant.

He knew why she was eager to leave, and he couldn't say he blamed her. The tension between them had become unbearable.

Even though he knew why she wanted to go, he sure as hell didn't have to like it. The idea of her living alone, unprotected, on that dark street with whoever had targeted her still on the loose appealed to him about as much as sticking his hand in a meat grinder.

He had argued fiercely, but she had stood firm. He had seen a completely unexpected stubborn light in her soft green eyes and had recognized the futility of pushing any harder.

The window installers were coming that day and she itched to get back to her gardens on her day off, she said. What did he expect her to do all day at his house alone?

He blew out a breath. He should have tried harder, but she had been right—what difference would it make if she spent the day alone at his house or alone at her own?

Finally he'd decided to let it ride, as long as she agreed to take Daisy with her for protection. The big dog could stand guard until the end of his shift, when he would take over. Though, of course, he neglected to fill Sarah in on that little detail of his plan.

Daisy was as gentle as a lamb, but her sheer size alone might deter any attacker and she also had moments of fierceness when the people she loved were threatened. One day the summer before, she had faced off against an angry bull at the Diamond Harte when Lucy had wandered into the wrong pasture by mistake. Since the dog had immediately taken Sarah into her big heart, he had no doubt she'd protect her any way she could.

Even with Daisy on guard duty, though, he couldn't shake his uneasiness.

Only part of this itch between his shoulder blades had to do with any hypothetical danger Sarah might be in. He had faced a few things in the middle of yet another night stirring and pacing down the hall from her. Things that scared him far more than punks who scrawled graffiti on her door.

He cared about Sarah McKenzie, in a way he never had about any other woman. Somehow her gentleness and her courage and her quiet beauty had reached right in and wrapped themselves around his heart.

He'd been hoping Corey would help take his mind off Sarah and these new terrifying feelings, but now he didn't even have that.

His stomach grumbled, reminding him he'd been too

busy arguing with her—and trying to fight the urge to quiet that soft mouth the very best way he could come up with—that he hadn't had time to grab anything to eat for breakfast.

There were usually bagels out by the coffeemaker, the healthier alternative to that old cop cliché, doughnuts. He walked out to check out his options and found Chris Hernandez standing at the desk talking through the security window to someone in the small waiting room.

The officer turned when she heard him approach. "Chief, the mayor's wife is here. For some reason, she seems to think she's supposed to be picking her son up here. Do you know anything about it?"

He frowned. So Corey had ditched him without his mother's knowledge. The little rascal. "I'll take care of it, Chris."

He walked up to the window to greet Ginny. She smiled brightly when she saw him and hitched Maddie higher on her hip. She was wearing one of those designer nylon workout suits and looked cool and stylish, except for the mushy crumbs on her shoulder from the cookie Maddie was flailing around in her chubby little hands.

Even with the crumbs, Ginny looked worlds away from the scared, defeated woman who had lived on Elk Mountain with Hob Sylvester.

"Hi, Jess. I'm here for Corey, but if the two of you aren't done, I'm happy to wait."

He hated having to pop that cheerful mood of hers, but her scamp of a son hadn't left him with much choice. "Corey's not here, Gin. He never showed."

Her bright smile trickled away like petals blown on a hard wind. "What do you mean, he never showed?

I dropped him off right in front of the police station more than an hour ago. I watched him walk in.''

''He must have waited until you drove away, then snuck right back out again. I'm sorry.''

She seemed to shrink, to crumple right in front of his eyes. ''I don't understand this. I thought he was really looking forward to your presentation. Why would he run off?''

''It's a nice day. Maybe he just wanted to go fishing or something.''

''Maybe.'' She didn't look convinced. Instead, she looked about ready to burst into tears any minute now.

Aw, hell. Just what he needed. He wasn't any good with crying women. ''Come on back and we can talk about it.'' He thumbed the security button for the door, then held it open for her. ''Here, let me take the rug rat.''

The baby felt soft and light in his arms, despite her chubby arms. She grinned at him, proudly displaying all four of her little teeth, and handed him her cookie.

''No, thanks,'' he said. ''Maybe later, sweetheart.''

Maddie seemed to think that was the most hilarious thing she'd ever heard. She let out a piercing squeal and bucked her whole body back and forth, forcing him to hold on tight so she didn't slip out of his arms.

''Whoa there, partner.'' He laughed and Maddie responded to it by giving another James Brown-like squeal and patting his cheeks with her sticky fingers.

''I'm sorry. She's such a mess.'' Now Ginny looked embarrassed *and* defeated.

''I'll wash.''

He didn't mind. Maddie was a doll, with her chubby cheeks and that curly blond hair and huge blue eyes. A quick memory of his niece Lucy when she was this age flitted through his mind—how she used to curl up on his lap with her thumb in her mouth and let him rock her to sleep.

He'd forgotten that. Lucy hadn't cared that he was a wild hell-raiser in those days—she had given him unconditional love anyway. To her, he was probably just the big, funny-looking guy who told silly jokes and tickled her cheeks with his razor stubble.

What would it be like to have one of these of his own?

The thought came out of the blue, just about knocking him on his butt. He had a sudden image of a giggly little girl with Sarah's honey-blond hair and big green eyes.

Yikes. Slow down. That kind of thinking could get a man in serious trouble.

"I'm so sorry about the mix-up," Ginny said when they reached his office. "I'm sure you had a million better things to do than sit here waiting for Corey to show."

He jerked his mind away from the weird, terrifying fantasies that had suddenly taken over. "It's no big deal. I'm just worried about him. Any clue where he might have gone?"

"No. How terrible is that for a mother to say? I have no idea where my son might be." Misery coated her voice. "Probably the same place he's been sneaking off to for the last few months."

"He's been doing a lot of this?"

"Two nights ago he climbed out his bedroom window and took off somewhere until after two in the morning. The only reason we knew he'd been gone is that Maddie woke up. When I got her settled back to sleep, I went to check on Corey and caught him climbing back through the window.''

"Did he say where he'd been?"

"Just hanging out with his friends. That's what he says, anyway. I don't know what to do anymore. We've taken away his bike and his scooter and his roller blades. He hasn't had TV or computer privileges in a month. Nothing we do is working. He's still sneaking out. Seth is talking about sending him to military school—this whole brand thing has been the last straw. Can you imagine a child doing such a thing to himself?"

"Maybe military school would be the best thing for him, just for a while. Until he straightens himself out."

Tears welled up in her eyes. "He's just a baby, Jess. Ten years old. It's a terrible thing to feel like you're losing your child."

He passed her his handkerchief and shifted Maddie in his arms, guilt tugging at him. He sure hadn't done a very good job of finding out what was happening with the kid. He'd thought they were making progress the few times they'd rehearsed, but Corey still clammed up every time Jesse tried to talk about anything other than their presentation.

"We'll find him, Gin. I've got two officers out in the field right now. I'll have them both keep an eye out for him and I'll hunt for him, too." They could look between their hourly patrols past Sarah's house. "We'll get to the bottom of it, I promise."

She sniffled into the handkerchief. "Thank you, Jess. Why do I always seem to end up dumping my problems on you?"

"I just wish you didn't have so many to deal with. You deserve to be happy."

Her chin wobbled a little. "Do I?"

"Yes. Of course! You've been through some rough times, but you've survived. You've made a great life for yourself, with a good, decent man. Hang in there. Corey will settle down. Look at me. I was a whole lot more wild than he could ever dream of being and I turned out okay."

She managed a watery grin. "That's a matter of opinion."

Maddie apparently thought that was the second funniest thing she'd ever heard. She let loose with another round of squealing giggles, showing off her tiny little teeth.

"See? She agrees with me."

This time Ginny's smile looked a little more natural, he was relieved to see. "I'd better take the little urchin home and get her washed up," she said. "Thanks Jess, for everything. I don't know what I'd do without you."

He rose along with her. "I'll carry Maddie out for you."

"You don't have to do that. I'm used to carrying her."

"Let me. I don't get to hold a sweet little thing like this very often."

"You need a family of your own. I've always thought you'd make a wonderful father."

He thought of that little girl he'd just imagined with Sarah's eyes and smile. The funny tug in the pit of his stomach just about made him break into a cold sweat.

He hid his reaction behind a casual grin. "No, thanks. I see Lucy and Dylan and all the mischief they get into, and then the grief that Corey's giving you right now, and it convinces me maybe I'm better off sticking with Daisy. At least she doesn't talk back to me much.''

Ginny's smile was bittersweet. ''Oh, Jess. Children might break your heart sometimes, but they bring far more joy than sorrow, even in the worst of times.''

''I'll have to take your word for that.''

They walked out of his office into the squad room and were nearly to the door when Ginny stopped behind him.

''Hey, why do you have Seth's favorite fishing cap? Did he leave it here? I swear, that husband of mine would lose his head if it wasn't screwed on.''

He froze, Maddie still squirming in his arms, and turned back to her. Ginny was holding the evidence bag containing the only link they had to the suspect in the vandalism at Sarah's house.

He thought of smeared blood and vicious messages and shattered windows. ''That hat belongs to Seth?'' he asked carefully, his heart pounding in a thick and sluggish away.

''Believe me, I wouldn't make a mistake about something like that. I've tried to burn the blasted thing several times. You'd think it was solid gold, for all the fuss Seth makes whenever I threaten to throw it away. He about pitched a fit when he couldn't find it last week. He'll be so glad to have it back.'' She reached to open the bag.

''Wait!''

His loud command made Ginny jump and Maddie giggle. His mind raced as he tried to process the information and figure out what to tell Ginny about the ugly suspicions that had suddenly taken root.

''Do you mind if I hang on to it for a while longer? I'd like to see his face when he gets it back. My officers

would enjoy playing a little joke on the mayor. You
know. Wrap it up and give it to him as a gift for, um,
giving us such a hard time about our budget.''

She shrugged. ''Sure. Anything to keep that stinky,
dirty old thing out of my house a little longer.''

He could think of nothing but the implications of
that cap belonging to Seth as he walked Ginny to her
Range Rover and buckled Maddie into her car seat in
the back.

He gave the little girl a distracted kiss, then kissed
Ginny on the forehead. ''I'll let you know if we find
Corey. If he comes home before you hear from me,
give me a buzz so I can call off my officers.''

''Thanks, Jess.'' Some of her cheerfulness had returned and she smiled and waved as she backed out of
the parking space and drove away.

He watched her go, his mind still racing. Could Seth
really have been involved with the vandalism at
Sarah's house? He thought about how upset the mayor
had been when he'd been accused of abusing Corey.
Could he have somehow found out Sarah was behind
the accusation? Was this a payback of some kind?

It didn't make sense. He had known Seth most of
his life, gone to Scout camp with him, double-dated in
high school. The man he knew couldn't possibly be
capable of such viciousness, could he?

But what other explanation could there be for his
cap being on the scene?

Somehow Corey was the link. He needed to find the
kid, sit him down and have a good long talk.

He was just sliding into his Bronco when his radio
buzzed with static. ''Chief, do you copy?'' Jim Lov-
ell's voice came over the airwaves along with a big
dose of static.

He reached for the mike. "Yeah, Jim. What's up?"

"You might want to get over here. Ron Atkins just found a body on his ranch. A woman's body."

His heart stopped beating, his vision dimmed around the edges. All he could think of was Sarah, alone at her house with just a dog for protection.

Sarah hummed along with the country song on the radio as she tore pieces of lettuce for her salad. It was a little late for lunch—after three—but she'd been too busy earlier in the day to eat.

Daisy sat at her feet, looking up every few minutes with a hopeful look in her big brown eyes.

"I don't think you'd like the salad, sweetie," she assured the dog, but slipped her a few pieces of cold chicken anyway. They disappeared with one big gulp and a plea for more, making her laugh.

She had spent a great morning puttering around in her garden. She had needed it after the night before, desperately craved the peace she found there. Having Daisy's gentle, uncomplicated company had only made the morning that much sweeter.

Maybe she ought to get a dog. A big, furry retriever just like Daisy to share her secrets with and talk to and draw comfort from on cold winter nights when she had no one else.

She sighed. She sounded pathetic, but she couldn't deny she felt much better today after pouring out her woes to the dog.

It's a good thing Daisy couldn't talk, or she would have an earful to give to Jesse about the silly woman who was afraid she might be falling in love with him.

She gave a rueful laugh. She wasn't kidding anybody, not even Daisy. She wasn't afraid, she was terrified. What's worse, there was no *maybe* about it. She was already there, head over heels in love with a man who wouldn't even touch her.

The doorbell rang suddenly, sounding unnaturally loud in the quiet house. Her heart jumped into her throat, no doubt in her mind as to who stood on her doorstep. Daisy had given it away, uttering just one excited bark then leaping for the front door, only to stand there with her tail wagging like a metronome on steroids.

Okay. Calm down, she ordered herself, and swung open the door. She could be cool and composed.

She wasn't at all prepared for the fury on his face, blazing at her like a furnace blast.

"Where the hell have you been?" He brushed past her and into the house, hand on his gun butt as if expecting a whole platoon of criminals to be sharing her Caesar salad.

She stiffened her spine at his tone. "I've been here all day, exactly as you ordered me this morning."

His glower turned even more forbidding. "Haven't you ever heard of answering the phone? I've been calling the whole damn afternoon."

"I've been outside in the yard. You wouldn't believe the weeds that took over in just a week..."

He cut her off with an oath far more pungent than the fertilizer she'd just finished spreading on her fledgling vegetables.

"You mean to tell me you didn't take a cordless phone outside with you?"

Her mouth pursed into a tight line. She wasn't about to let him stand here in her house and yell at her as if she were a fractious child. "I don't recall that being among the lengthy list of commands you left me with this morning. Did I miss one?''

"It's called common sense.''

Her eyes widened. "Excuse me?''

"Until we know who's nursing one serious grudge against you, I don't want to take any chances with your safety.''

"I was perfectly safe. I kept Daisy with me the entire time.''

"How was I supposed to know that when you didn't answer the damn phone? You have any idea how worried I've been?''

Now that she looked more closely, she could see the lines of strain around his mouth, the dark shadows in his eyes. *He was worried about her.* Most of her annoyance at his sharp tone began to fade away, replaced by a slow, steady warmth that leapt to life in her chest.

"I'm sorry,'' she murmured. "But as you can see, you worried for nothing. I'm perfectly fine. Great, even.''

He pulled his brown police-issue Stetson off and raked a hand through his dark hair. "Small consolation that is when I haven't been able to concentrate on anything but you all afternoon. If I could have broken away from the crime scene any earlier, I would have been here hours ago to check on you.''

"Crime scene?''

He shrugged. "A rancher found some bones on a remote area of his property, just inside the city limits. We called in the Wyoming State Police and they'll do most of the investigative work, but I still had to secure the scene.''

"Do they think it was murder?''

"Too early to say until the state forensics lab has a

chance to do its thing. All we know is that it was a woman, judging by the clothing found on the scene, and she's been there a while. Other than that, we don't have much to go on.''

He paused for a moment, then narrowed his gaze dangerously. ''And you're not going to distract me that easily. You wouldn't believe the kinds of things that raced through my head when I couldn't get through. Don't scare me like that again.''

The concern in his voice, in those glittering blue eyes, made her suddenly, abashedly, weepy. ''I'm sorry. I didn't think. I was just so happy to be out in the garden again.''

He continued watching her, a strange light in his eyes. ''Your nose is sunburned.''

That's where the sting must be coming from. She touched a finger to it, then felt a matching blush take over the rest of her skin. Why was he looking at her like that?

''Um, I was just making a salad. Chicken Caesar. There's more than enough for two if you'd like to stay.''

''I'd rather kiss you again.''

She froze in place, her gaze darting to his as she felt her face flame even hotter.

''Don't look so surprised.'' He parroted her words of the day before. ''I'm sure half the men in town would love to do the same.''

''But not you, obviously,'' she muttered, then stopped, mortified that she'd given voice to her thoughts.

His laugh was short and held little amusement. ''You've got to be kidding. I haven't been able to think about anything else for days.''

"You don't have to lie, Jesse." She dug her fists into Daisy's fur, refusing to meet that blue gaze. "I don't blame you for not finding me attractive after learning what…what happened in Chicago."

"Not finding you attractive?" He growled an oath. "You don't have a clue, do you?"

"About what?"

"I could be crude and show you exactly what happens to me just being in the same room as you, but I'll refrain."

She stared at him, stunned, and he blew out a ragged-sounding breath. "Sarah, I think you are without question the most beautiful, courageous, incredible woman I've ever met. You're like a soft, slender willow, bowed by the wind but not broken by it, and I've been *attracted* to you—as you so mildly put it—since the day you moved to Star Valley."

A slow heat began to blossom inside her at his words. She felt shaky and aroused and very, very touched. So touched that she had to swallow hard twice before she could get the words out. "Why did you stop last night, then?"

He stepped forward and traced a thumb down her cheek. The tenderness of it brought tears to her eyes. "Oh, sweetheart. Not because I didn't want you. It took every ounce of strength I could find to step away."

"But you did step away."

"Because I knew that if I touched you again, kissed you again, I would make love to you."

"I wanted you to." She swallowed hard once more, trying to gather that courage he claimed she had. At last she managed to summon enough to meet his gaze. "I still want you to."

Chapter 12

He closed his eyes, her words slicing through him like a hot blade, and dropped his hand from her skin. He couldn't touch her right now. Not when his control teetered on a razor-thin edge.

"Sarah, I can't."

He heard her shaky intake of air and opened his eyes to find her features had become a still, fragile mask.

"Okay. I guess we know where we stand." She stepped away from him, and his heart broke a little.

He wouldn't let her retreat. Not like this. He gripped her hands in his and found them cool and trembling.

"Listen to me, sweetheart. Stopping the other night was the hardest thing I've ever done in my life, but I had no choice. I was too close to losing control. Too hungry for you. If it scared the hell out of me, I could only imagine what it would do to you. I couldn't take the risk of frightening you. "

"Because I was raped."

She said it as a statement, not a question. He blew out a breath. "I hate that it happened to you. I would give anything I own to change the past, to be able to go back and protect you from it somehow."

"You can't, though," she said. "It *did* happen to me and it's part of who I am now."

Her hands grew still in his and she met his gaze. He was stunned by the jumbled mix of emotions swimming there, but he also recognized desire when he saw it.

"I'm so tired of being afraid. Tired of feeling numb and timid and half-dead all the time. I feel alive with you, Jesse. Wonderfully alive. And very, very safe."

How was he supposed to find the strength to walk away after she said a thing like that? "Sarah—"

"You won't hurt me, Jess. I know you would die before you would ever hurt me." Her low voice strummed along his spine and he suddenly couldn't seem to draw enough air into his lungs.

He couldn't walk away. Not after this.

He murmured her name again, then cupped her sweet, beautiful face in his hands and kissed her gently.

She sighed against his mouth and settled in his arms as if she belonged nowhere else.

This was what she wanted. Dear heavens, this was exactly what she wanted. Sarah nestled against him, loving the strength of his arms around her, the solid expanse of chest beneath her hands. This hard, dangerous man cared about her—she had seen the truth in his eyes. How could she ever be frightened of that?

She loved him. Loved him and wanted to be here with him, with every shimmering, buzzing cell in her body.

"You'll tell me if I do anything you don't like," he

commanded. "If I touch you wrong or startle you or anything at all."

Laughter bubbled up in her chest. Who would have believed it? The heartbreaker of Star Valley was more nervous about this than she was! "I swear," she said, managing to choke down her giggle. "You'll be the first to know."

He kissed her again, long and hard and full of promise, until she just about melted all over the floor of her living room.

"We're not doing this here." He drew back, his voice hoarse. "I don't need a damn audience."

She glanced down and found Daisy watching them with interest, her tail wagging as she moved her head back and forth between the two of them like an observer at a Ping-Pong tournament.

Sarah laughed out loud this time, full of joy and tenderness and that wondrous thrum of anticipation. "My bedroom. Through the hall, second door on the right."

Her laughter changed to a gasp when he effortlessly lifted her into his arms and carried her through the house to her room, closed the door with his boot and set her gently on the bed.

"Promise me, Sarah. Promise you'll tell me if you're at all uncomfortable."

She nodded slowly, their gazes locked together. "As long as you promise you won't hold back."

He stood watching her for a long time, until hot color soaked her skin in a slow glide from cheeks to neck to breasts. Then he leaned down and kissed her with soft, aching tenderness.

"I promise." He whispered the vow against her mouth and she breathed it inside her.

She wrapped her arms around him, pulling him closer, and he deepened the kiss, explored her mouth until she was wet and weak and trembling. She gasped when his lips slid away from hers and began trailing kisses down the column of her neck.

"You taste like sunlight." He nipped another taste. "Sunlight and flowers."

She watched him, breathless and aroused and suddenly embarrassed. "I've been out working in the garden all day. It's probably more like sweat and fertilizer."

"Let's see." He glided his mouth down the column of her throat, to the buttons of her faded denim work shirt. She found it unbearably sexy watching his hands—broad and strong and masculine—as he worked each button. And even more sexy when his mouth followed the pathway of those hands, pressing soft, barely there kisses in a long trail down the strip of skin revealed by each undone button.

After dipping his tongue into her navel, he slid up and caught her mouth with his again. "Nope. Definitely flowers," he murmured.

He slid aside the edges of her shirt, then worked the front clasp of her bra with a skill she might have teased him about under other circumstances. Now she could only watch him, her breath tangled in her throat as he freed her breasts from the lacy cups.

She wasn't very well endowed in that area. He was probably used to chesty women who knew how to flaunt their advantages, she thought glumly. Before she could come up with some kind of dismissive joke about it, her gaze met his and the stunned masculine appreciation in those dark blue depths sent her pulse rate skyrocketing.

He whispered a prayer or an oath—she wasn't sure which—then pressed his mouth reverently first to one slope then the other.

She made a low, strangled noise in her throat and he quickly looked up. "Everything okay?"

She couldn't talk just now. Not with this aching tenderness in her throat, this heavy ache in her breasts, in her womb. She decided this was one of those times when words weren't necessary anyway, so she gripped his hair tightly and drew his head back to her.

His laugh sounded rough against her breasts, but his mouth was gentle. His lips settled over one jutting peak, drawing it slowly into his mouth. She still hadn't found her breath when he began removing the rest of her clothing, then his own.

Distracted by the slow, heated magic of his mouth on her skin, she was hardly aware of it until he stood before her.

She blinked, stunned. He was beautiful. Ruggedly, unashamedly male, with a sculpted chest tapering to a lean waist, skin stretched taut over hard muscles. Her eyes dipped lower and she blushed bright red at the evidence of his desire.

"Don't look at me like that," he ordered roughly.

"Like what?"

"Like I'm the big bad wolf about to gobble you up."

"Promises, promises," she murmured, and had the very distinct pleasure of seeing his eyes go wide and unfocused with desire.

He joined her on the bed again and she had to close her eyes as sensation after sensation washed over her at the intimacy of being there with him.

He kissed her again, his mouth gentle as his hands explored her skin with slow, sensual movements. She sighed against his mouth. She loved the way he was touching her, but something was wrong. It took her a moment to figure out what. He was treating her like some kind of fragile porcelain doll, not like a woman.

She wanted more. She wanted to taste that wildness in him. Wanted heat and strength and passion, not this careful deference.

Frustrated, yearning, she reached between their bodies and closed her fingers around him. He froze with a harsh intake of breath, impaling her with his gaze. The raw desire there was everything she could have asked for and more.

"Be careful," he warned, sending shivers of anticipation rippling down her spine.

"I'm tired of being careful. I won't break, Jesse. I promise."

Her words seemed to unlock some kind of dam inside him. His movements became urgent, hurried. He licked, nipped, tasted her skin, while his long fingers played at the apex of her thighs.

She was more than ready for him, wet and slick and eager. She wanted him, wanted this. Still, she tensed when she felt his hard strength *there* preparing to enter her. A thin edge of nerves suddenly crackled through her like heat lightning and she jerked back.

She muttered a curse, furious with herself. She wasn't afraid. Damn it, she wouldn't be nervous. This was Jesse, and she trusted him completely.

"Sarah, look at me," he ordered. She obeyed, her breath coming hard and fast as she tried to stay in control.

The tenderness in his blue eyes, on those gorgeous hard features, almost made her weep. He framed her face with his hands. "It's okay. We'll take things slow for now. There's plenty of time for more later if you want to. And if you don't—if you're not ready—that's okay, too.''

''No. Please, Jess. I want this.''

He studied her for a moment, looking for any indication her words held more bravado than she was really feeling. Apparently satisfied, he slid between her legs again and entered her slowly, carefully.

She held her breath and kept her eyes open, her gaze locked with his. This was right. Oh, sweet heaven, this was right. She felt as if she were floating along on a sweet, warm river of need and it was wonderful.

Exercising great care and restraint, he moved inside her subtly, just enough that she gasped. The easy current of desire eddying around her churned a little faster, a little wilder, and she clutched at him.

He kissed her, blue eyes still wide open and burning into hers. ''It's okay,'' he murmured against her mouth. ''Don't be afraid. I promise, I'll stop if you want me to.''

If he stopped, she would drown. She knew it as surely as she knew she loved him. These warm, erotic waves would change to the icy sea where she usually floated and she would sink below the frigid depths.

She couldn't find the words to tell him, so she used her mouth, her hands, her body.

She saw the need haze his eyes, felt his movements become more urgent. Finally, when she thought she wouldn't be able to bear this sweet tension another instant, he reached between their bodies and touched her.

Slick heat poured through her as she gasped his name and together they plunged over the edge of a churning, sparkling, beautiful waterfall.

Then he held her while she gave in to the tears of relief and amazement and sweet, healing peace.

She was officially a fallen woman.

Sarah smiled a little as she turned the lights off in her classroom late Monday afternoon.

All day, through math and spelling and social studies, she had been able to think of nothing but Jesse and waking this morning in his strong arms.

They had shared an incredible weekend, much of it in bed. After a quick trip back to his house Sunday morning for clothes and food for poor, hungry Daisy, they had cooked breakfast together in her little kitchen, laughing like a pair of kids making mud pies even as they paused frequently for more of those long, intoxicating kisses that turned her knees to spaghetti.

They ate breakfast in her bed and barely made it through the omelettes before she was in his arms once more. The kisses had led to touches, the touches to more.

Later she put him to work in her backyard, digging and pruning and hauling. She had this idea for a goldfish pond in the corner and had roped him into helping. It was no real hardship, she had to admit, watching him wield a shovel with those powerful muscles flexing under his shirt.

Jesse had a standing command performance for Sunday dinner at the Diamond Harte when he wasn't on duty. Despite her protests, he had insisted on taking her along.

She smiled a little, remembering the reaction of his family. She had feared it might be awkward for them to have her as an unexpected guest, but the girls had been ecstatic at the prospect of sharing dinner with their teacher.

She had the feeling Jesse didn't usually bring someone to the family gatherings—Ellie and Jesse's older brother, Matt, hadn't quite managed to conceal their surprise—but they had been warm and welcoming.

Cassie had just grinned at her.

It had been wonderful to see the easy, teasing affection in the family. She had missed this growing up as an only child, the banter and the stories and the easy, loving familiarity.

Though she knew the danger of it, she couldn't help wondering what it would be like to belong, to be a part of this tight-knit family.

She wasn't stupid enough to think what she and Jesse shared could ever be a forever kind of thing. What could she—a dowdy mouse of a schoolteacher, afraid of her own shadow—hope to offer a man as vibrant and alive as Jesse Harte?

For some mysterious reason, he was attracted to her. Any doubts she might have entertained about that had been dispelled about the seventh or eighth time he had reached hungrily for her over the weekend.

But she knew it wouldn't last.

She hadn't told him she loved him. A few times she had come close to whispering it as she had rested beside him with her cheek against his warm skin, listening to the steady comfort of his heartbeat. But she had swallowed the words down, knowing he wouldn't want them. Knowing they would only make him uncomfortable.

Her sigh stirred the air. She had gone into this with her eyes wide open. She knew from the beginning Jesse wasn't a forever kind of man, so she had determined to squeeze every ounce of joy from this time and store it up in her heart.

For this moment, he was hers. She wasn't going to spoil it by regretting the impossible.

Besides, how could she be depressed when a man like Jesse Harte—with his hands and his strength and his devastating smile—would be on his way to meet her within the hour?

She reached the outside door of the school and unfurled her umbrella, with its print of one of Monet's water lily series.

It had started to rain the night before, a wild, noisy, flashing storm that battered the new windows of her little cottage. She and Jesse hadn't minded. They'd been snug inside, tangled together under her thick comforter.

By morning, the violent weather had changed to a soft, steady rain that hadn't eased all day. Her class had been forced to endure all three recesses inside, and she had done her best to keep her restless, ready-for-summer students entertained with seven-up and desk baseball and computer games.

Only a few more weeks and the school term would end. Every year she promised herself she wouldn't get emotional at the end of the year and every year she did. She would miss her students when they moved on to fifth grade. The only consolation she could find was that in a few months she would have thirty more children to love.

Her shoes were soaked by the time she reached her car. She unlocked her door, shook the water off her umbrella and started to close it when she heard the low rumble of an approaching vehicle.

Somebody else working late, she thought. Or maybe

Jesse coming to check on her. The thought warmed her deep inside and she turned with a ready smile. It slid away at the sight of a dilapidated, mud-splattered pickup truck.

The driver was a stranger, a man around Jesse's age. Through the rain sluicing down his windshield she could see a long, drooping mustache and dirty blond hair receding off a high forehead.

He definitely wasn't a teacher. Maybe he was a new custodian or a parent looking for a late student.

She gave a quick, impersonal smile, and was about to slide into her car when he opened his door and called her name on a question.

With a sudden vague foreboding she stood with the door of her own car open and one foot inside. Her upholstery would be drenched in this rain, but she didn't care. Even though she knew it was silly, she suddenly needed the security of her vehicle.

"Yes," she said, with a calmness she didn't feel. "I'm Sarah McKenzie."

"I'd like to talk to you about my kid. He's in your class."

She frowned, even more uneasy. After an entire school term, she thought she knew the parents of every single student in her class, but she definitely didn't remember this man. "I'm sorry. I think you're mistaken. Are you sure I'm your child's teacher?"

"Yeah." He climbed out of the truck and walked over to her, his hand outstretched. He had thick, beefy fingers and a build to match. Definitely someone she didn't want to mess with. "Name's Hob Sylvester. My boy, Corey, has been in your class for a few months."

Corey Sylvester? She knew Seth was the boy's step-father, but she had no idea Corey's real father even lived in Wyoming, let alone in Star Valley. This was the first she'd ever heard of him.

Knowing his identity should have allayed her misgivings, but she still felt an icy prickle under her skin that had nothing to do with the rain. "It's terrible weather out here and the school is closed, Mr. Sylvester. Why don't we make an appointment tomorrow right after school to talk?"

He studied her for a moment, then twisted his lips into a cold smile. "No. I'd rather talk now."

Her uneasiness blossomed into full-fledged panic. Her gaze skittered around the virtually empty parking lot, to the darkened school. A few people might still be inside, but they would never hear her call for help from clear out here.

They were completely alone and the knowledge suddenly terrified her.

"We can talk tomorrow." She slid into her car, heedless at how rude she might appear to a parent of one of her students, or how foolish she would probably feel later, when she was safe and warm and dry in her own house, in Jesse's arms.

All she could focus on now was the sudden panic spurting through her. Adrenaline surged in her veins and she yanked the door closed behind her and fumbled with the locks.

She wasn't fast enough. Before she could engage them, the man yanked the door open.

"Don't you want to talk to me?" His voice was more like a snarl now. "I thought teachers were always complaining about parents not being interested in their kids' education. Well, I'm interested, so let's talk."

He loomed over her, large and menacing. All he wanted to do was talk, she assured herself. Just talk.

What was the harm in that? It helped her regain control a little.

"I'm sorry, Mr. Sylvester. I'm late for an appointment," she lied. "Please come to school tomorrow." She heard the pleading note in her voice and hated it, but couldn't manage to keep it out.

"My daddy always said, why do tomorrow what you can do today?"

His eyes looked wild, something she hadn't noticed before, and she picked up the strong, fiery smell of hard liquor on his breath. Five in the afternoon and the man was stinking drunk.

Without warning, he suddenly grabbed her arm and tugged her from the car with one hand. In his other, a stubby black handgun appeared out of nowhere.

At the sight of it, her mind went completely blank, like a vast field of blinding new snow.

No. Please, God. No.

This couldn't be happening to her again.

"Come on, teacher. You and me are gonna take a little ride."

His grip on her arm tightened and her vision grayed around the edges. The flashback punched her hard in the stomach.

Suddenly she wasn't in the parking lot of Salt River Elementary anymore, with the comforting mountains around her and the rain drizzling steadily down. She was once more in her classroom in Chicago, with Tommy DeSilva hitting her, ripping at her clothes, on top of her.

The scream built in her throat, died there. No. She blinked hard, using every ounce of strength she possessed to choke down the memories. She had to stay in control, stay focused.

Jesse would find her. When she wasn't at home as he expected, he would come to the school and see her car. He would immediately know something was wrong, and he would find her.

She had to help him. To send some kind of message, a clue where to start looking for her.

She took a deep breath, again fighting down the panic that crouched like a snarling beast inside her. Think, she ordered herself, clutching her bag more tightly in her hand.

Her bag! She had been taking home a stack of reports on the California gold rush to grade, and Corey's paper was right at the front of the stack. She remembered, because she'd been so pleased and surprised that he had actually bothered to turn in an assignment.

While the man yanked her toward the truck, she managed to hitch the bag to her shoulder so she could use her free hand to reach inside. Her fist closed over the report she had to pray was Corey's. As Hob Sylvester struggled to shove her into the truck, he didn't notice at all when she dropped the report and her bag where she hoped Jesse would find them.

As a clue, it wasn't much—obscure, at best—but she would have to trust that Jesse would understand.

Inside the old pickup she nearly gagged at the stench, of stale sweat and spoiled milk and the sick, yeasty scent of old beer. It was filthy, covered in fast-food wrappers and crushed beer cans and used tissues. On the passenger seat was a pile of empty paper coin rolls and what looked suspiciously like a pair of women's underwear.

Hob Sylvester swept them all to the floor, then shoved her in.

The only way she would get through this was to keep

her wits about her. "What did you want to talk to me about?" she asked woodenly, as if this were just another parent-teacher conference.

He chortled as he elbowed the floor gearshift. The truck lurched obediently forward. "We can talk about anything you want, darlin'. We could talk about Corey's grades or the damn price of tea in China or how you're gonna help me get back what's mine."

He smiled and she had the strange thought that with those striking green eyes he had probably been handsome once. Now the eyes were bloodshot, his mouth hard.

In the side mirror she could see the school building recede into the distance as they drove through the rain. Panic began to chew at her again, but she pushed it away.

"You know this is kidnapping, don't you? You're taking me against my will."

He snorted. "I might not be a smart schoolteacher like you, but I'm not completely stupid. I know exactly what I'm doing."

"This is a serious offense, Mr. Sylvester. Why don't you let me go and we can pretend this never happened? I won't tell anyone."

"Because I've got plans for you, teacher. Big plans."

She drew a deep, shuddering breath. She couldn't think about it. Jesse would find her. She knew he would. He had to.

Corey's father picked up a bottle still in the paper bag and took a long swig, then wiped at his mouth. If he were drunk, he might be careless. She would have to pray she could find a way to escape.

"Where are we going?" she asked, striving with everything she had to keep her voice casual.

"A place where nobody can hear what I'm gonna do to you."

His smile didn't come close to reaching his eyes. This time she could no longer keep the panic at bay. It snarled once, then lunged for her and swallowed her whole.

Man, he had it bad.

He hated to admit it, but Matt had been right. After dinner the night before, his know-it-all big brother had taken him outside on the pretext of showing off one of his new mares.

Eventually—as he realized now Matt intended all along—the conversation had drifted to what the hell he thought he was doing messing around with a nice woman like Sarah McKenzie.

Before he could get huffy about his big brother's insulting tone, Matt had taken one look at him and ended up poleaxing Jesse with the truth.

Jesse James Harte, the bad boy of Salt River, Wyoming, was head over heels in love with a sweet, quiet schoolteacher.

He'd damn near punched his brother in the face at the time. It couldn't be true. He cared about her—wanted to keep her safe and make her smile—and he was definitely attracted to her gentle, willowy beauty, but he couldn't be in love with her.

Throughout a day spent chewing it over, though, he'd been chagrined to realize Matt had been right. It burned his gut worse than Cassie's hot chili to admit that his nosy older brother had recognized Jesse's feelings for Sarah before he did.

But how could he have realized it when he didn't have any kind of frame of reference to measure his feelings against? He'd never been in love before. Never even come close.

He'd always figured there was something lacking in him, some cold empty place inside where something good must have died the day his parents did. Or maybe it had just shriveled away in those wild, rowdy years after.

But now that he'd been knocked over the head with the truth, he couldn't deny it. He was in love with Sarah McKenzie. He had a feeling he'd been on his way there since the day she came to Salt River.

Now, as he drove toward the school to meet her, he was amazed at the anticipation thrumming through him. It hadn't even been twelve hours since he'd left her warm, flower-scented bed and he couldn't wait to see her again. To touch that soft skin. To watch her eyes go hazy with need, to see that smile sneak out of nowhere—that sweet smile that always seemed to reach right into his chest and yank out his heart.

He was in love with her. Now, what the hell was he supposed to do about it?

For the first time in his life, he was thinking about more than just having a good time. He was thinking about forever kinds of things—happily-ever-after kinds of things. Marriage, kids, the whole works.

And trying to ignore the snide little voice inside him that he couldn't seem to make shut up, the voice reminding him that he didn't even come close to deserving a woman as good and decent as Sarah.

He gripped the steering wheel a little tighter, eyes straight ahead. He didn't want to think about that now.

About his past and the things he'd done. He didn't want any of that touching her, ever.

A few blocks from the school, an older rattletrap of a pickup passed him, its huge gas-guzzling engine growling through the late afternoon. He didn't recognize the truck and couldn't see much of the driver through the rain, but he waved anyway. This was Salt River. It would have been rude not to.

A few moments later, he pulled into the school parking area and saw with relief that Sarah's sage Toyota was one of only a handful of cars in the parking lot. Good. Looked as if his hunch was right, to come here instead of her house. Even with the school year winding down, Sarah still put in long, hard hours at her job.

He admired her dedication and wondered again where he would have been if one of his teachers had taken the interest in him that she did with all her pupils.

Though it was still an hour or so from sunset, the gunmetal-gray storm clouds made it seem much darker and later. He looked for Sarah's classroom windows, but didn't see any lights on inside. That didn't mean anything. Maybe she had a faculty meeting or was busy in the library.

He didn't mind waiting. It would give him a chance to figure out how to deal with this tangle of emotions twisting through him.

He started to pull in next to her car when his headlights caught on something lying in a puddle a few feet away. Some kid had probably dropped his backpack in a hurry to catch the bus and get home to his Nintendo. He should pick it up before the rain ruined it, if he wasn't too late.

With his engine still running, he climbed out to retrieve the thing. It wasn't a backpack, he discovered as he neared the puddle. He crouched and reached for it, then stopped when he recognized the tapestry floral print.

He'd seen Sarah walking out the door with this very bag earlier that morning.

What would her tote be doing out here in the rain? He frowned, unease suddenly crawling down his spine like a furry spider. She wouldn't have left it out in the rain. Not a chance. She was much too careful for that.

Leaving the bag, he walked to her car, and that one little prickle of unease became a whole damn nest of spiders skittering all over him at what he found. Her umbrella, the fancy flowery one he'd kissed her beneath that morning before she left her house, lay closed but not snapped on the ground.

Even more ominous, the car wasn't locked and he could see her keys in a jumbled heap on the seat.

What was going on here? The bag, the umbrella, the keys. They were here, but where the hell was Sarah?

Maybe she'd forgotten something and gone back into the school. But why would she leave her keys and her umbrella out here in the middle of a downpour, especially when he knew the school was always locked at this time of the afternoon?

He was about to bang on the door and scour the building for her when he spied something else in the puddle, a glimmer of white underneath her bag that he'd missed before. He lifted the sopping mess, which turned out to be some kind of homework assignment.

As soon as he read the student's name scrawled in uneven letters at the top, he knew instinctively that Sarah hadn't left this paper separate from the rest by accident. It was a clue to tell him where to find her.

She was in trouble, and it was somehow linked to Corey Sylvester.

Cold, stinging fear clutched his stomach. Could Seth have gotten to her somehow? Damn. He should have put some kind of protection on her. He'd thought they'd have more time before Garrett found out he was under investigation for the shattered windows at her house, the bloody warnings to mind her own business, the attempted break-in a few weeks earlier.

He hadn't arranged protection for her, though, mainly because he was still having a tough time believing Seth could be involved. He had a possible motive—anger at her for accusing him of hurting Corey—but Jesse wasn't convinced he had the personality for revenge.

He'd been working hard to come up with an alternative theory that made sense to explain why the mayor's favorite fishing cap had been found at the scene of a pretty sick crime. Coincidence? Mistake? A plant of some kind?

But how could he argue with this paper staring right back at him? Sarah was in trouble, he could feel it like a deep ache in his bones. What kind of trouble, he didn't know, but the trail led him right back to Seth Garrett.

What would the son of a bitch hope to gain? He didn't know and he couldn't wait around here to figure it out. His heart pounded out a fierce rhythm as he rushed to the Bronco and sped off through the gathering darkness. On the way to the Garretts, he radioed for an officer to search the school grounds and double-check her house, just in case he was wrong and she was safe and sound somewhere.

Even as he gave the order, he knew she wasn't.

Something was wrong. She needed him and this time he couldn't fail.

He didn't bother knocking at the Garretts', just shoved open the unlocked door.

Seth stood poised at the base of the stairs, as if he were just on his way up. Surprise flickered on his face at the intrusion, but Jesse didn't give him a chance to say a word. With adrenaline pumping through him like an uncapped oil well, he grabbed two fistfuls of beige golf shirt and rammed the other man against the wall so hard Seth's head connected with an ugly-sounding crack.

"You son of a bitch. Where is she?" Jesse barely recognized the rough, feral voice coming from his throat

In contrast, Seth's voice came out strangled. "Who? Ginny? She's in the kitchen."

He gave the man another hard shake. "Where's Sarah? What have you done to her?"

Seth's eyes widened. "Sarah McKenzie? Corey's teacher? I barely know the woman."

"You know her enough to stalk her. To lurk outside her house and smash in her windows and leave nasty notes on the door." He shook again. "I know you took her. Now, where is she?"

"You're crazy! I don't know what you're talking about, Jesse. I swear it."

Drawn by the raised voices, Ginny rushed into the entry. "Jesse! What is going on? Let him go!"

"Stay out of this, Gin."

"No. Good heavens, Jesse. What's gotten into you?"

"Is she here at the house? Are you hiding her in your garage?"

"Hiding who?" Ginny fluttered her hands. "This is ridiculous!"

"Sarah McKenzie is missing. And the only one I know in Salt River who might have a grudge against her is your husband."

"You're nuts." Seth's voice came out raspy. "What kind of grudge would I have against her? Corey's done better in just a few weeks spent in her class than he has all year!"

"How about retaliation for having your good name smeared by allegations of child abuse? You found out she's the one who made the accusation, didn't you?"

Seth's astonishment was either completely genuine or he had a lock on winning best actor of the century. "I had no idea who made the complaint until you just said it. I wouldn't have cared anyway, since it was completely false. I would never hurt Corey or Sarah McKenzie. Come on, Jess. You know me! You know I couldn't do any of this!"

The stunned sincerity in his expression, in his voice, gave Jesse the first flickers of doubt since he'd seen that soggy piece of paper with Corey's name on it. He suddenly realized he was a few moments away from strangling one of his oldest friends.

Could he have made a mistake?

He could barely see through the black haze of rage and worry consuming him at the thought of the nightmare Sarah must be going through. But he considered himself fairly good at reading people, and right now Seth looked stunned.

Jesse reluctantly released his hold and Seth slumped to a pine bench against the wall, rubbing his throat. "What's this about, Jess? Why would you think I'm involved?"

He raked a hand through his hair. What was he supposed to do now? He had to find her and couldn't afford to waste time here with explanations if Seth wasn't involved. What had she been trying to tell him by leaving that damn paper out of her bag?

"You heard about the vandalism at her house?"

"Yes. Betty Ann, my secretary, told me. She heard it from her sister Janie, who works with Sarah at the school. It sounded like a real mess."

"We found something of yours on the scene. We have reason to believe it was left there by whoever did the dirty work. I had a theory that it might be some kind of twisted revenge thing, but maybe it was just a plant. Something to throw us off."

"It wasn't me, I swear it."

Frustration prowled through him, gnawed at him. He wanted to pound his fist against the wall, to smash every single one of Ginny's pretty little knickknacks in the room.

Where was Sarah?

"Somehow her disappearance is linked to Corey. I can feel it in my bones. She left one of his homework assignments out of her bag. It was the only one she pulled out and I know she had to mean something by that. But what? Where the hell can she be?"

He heard a small sound above his head, like the mew of a tiny kitten, and Jesse jerked his gaze to the stairs. Corey stood halfway down, his hand on the railing and his face so pale his freckles stood out in sharp relief.

Ginny stepped forward. "Corey, do you know something about this?"

"Maybe." His usual screw-you attitude was nowhere in sight. Instead, he just looked like exactly what he was, a young boy—and a frightened one at that.

"What do you know?" his mother asked, when he didn't say anything more.

He swallowed hard and gripped the railing. "You'll be mad if I tell you."

Seth started up the stairs and laid a hand on the boy's shoulder. "Son, you have to tell what you know. Ms. McKenzie might be in danger."

Tears welled up in his eyes. "I didn't think he'd hurt her."

"Who, Corey?" Jesse pounced on him. "Where is she?"

"You could try Elk Mountain," he whispered

They all stared at him. "What?" Jesse growled.

"The trailer on Elk Mountain. Where we used to live."

Ginny hissed in a breath, her face going as pale as her son's. "What are you talking about? That trailer's abandoned. It's just a pile of junk. Why would Sarah possibly go there?"

"I don't know. But if she's missing, I think maybe my dad might have taken her there. That's where he's been living." Tears welled up in the boy's frightened eyes. "I'm sorry I didn't tell you he was back, Mom. He made me promise not to. Said he'd hurt Maddie or you if I told."

Hob Sylvester. Son of a bitch. Suddenly Corey's mysterious injuries these past few weeks made a whole lot more sense. "Why would Hob want to hurt Sarah? He doesn't even know her."

Corey sniffled. "I don't know. He was real mad at her, though. Said she should mind her own business after she had to go and tell 'bout the, um, the thing on my back."

"He...your father did that to you?" Ginny asked weakly.

Corey looked guilty and miserable at the same time. "When I told him about Seth wanting to adopt me, he got real mad. Said I was a Sylvester and he wouldn't let me ever forget it."

Jesse didn't wait to hear the rest. He was already heading for the door, a ragged curse on his tongue. Hob Sylvester. He thought of all the calls he'd responded to over the years on Elk Mountain, back when Ginny and Corey lived there. The bruises and the broken bones and the wounds that went far deeper than flesh.

Hob was a crazy, vindictive bully who was capable of anything. Just thinking about his sweet Sarah in the hands of a man like that sent a hot, greasy ball of fear slicking through him.

He had to hurry.

This time—please, God, this time—he wouldn't be too late.

"Here we are. End of the road, Teach."

Sarah tried not to listen to the voice. She was in a safe, warm place where no one could touch her—no one could scare her—and she couldn't let anyone disturb her.

She breathed deeply, shoving the entire weight of her psyche against the door to the terrifying world outside. If only she tried hard enough, she could keep that door closed tightly and could stay right here in this nice, safe, blank nothingness.

"Come on. I ain't got all day." Someone on the outside grabbed her arm and yanked her out of both the truck and her safe, private haven.

She wobbled a little at the impact of her abrupt return to earth.

"Come on," Corey's father said, his voice harsh and ugly.

He gripped her arm and started dragging her toward the only structure in sight among the towering trees, a dilapidated trailer with peeling aluminum skin of some nondescript color.

No. This wasn't right. She was supposed to be at her safe little cottage right now with Jesse, not at some junk heap in the middle of nowhere.

"I want to go home," she muttered.

"Tough," he snapped. He shoved her hard up the wooden steps. They were wet from the rain and she stumbled on a loose board. She reached a hand to the rickety railing to steady herself, then gasped as splinters drove into her skin.

The sharp pain brought her fully back to the grim reality of her situation. She was on an isolated mountainside with a man who appeared to be drunk at best, completely crazy at worst. Even if Jesse somehow miraculously managed to figure out where they'd gone, it still could be hours before he arrived for her.

She was going to have to save herself.

The idea just about sent her scurrying back to the safe place inside her head.

The flimsy door to the structure wasn't locked and Sylvester shoved her inside. Could he actually live here? It was little better than one of those cardboard boxes the homeless used back in Chicago.

It looked as if someone had tried to make the trailer a home at one time, but the wallpaper was stained with water, the lace curtains tattered and ripped.

Her gaze landed on something familiar. It appeared

she'd just solved the mystery of the school's missing coins. The shattered jar lay in a corner in thick broken shards amid a pile of coins.

So Chuck Hendricks had been right—Corey had been involved in the theft. Or at least his father had been.

She didn't have time to dwell on it. Sylvester shoved her toward a blue-and-gold couch missing most of its stuffing.

Still holding the gun, he immediately reached for yet another bottle on the counter, this one already half-empty, and carried it to the only other piece of furniture in the room, a chair of the same ugly print.

For a few moments he drank and muttered, some disjointed soliloquy about Seth and Ginny and Corey, about how Seth was going to pay for taking from Hob Sylvester. About how the stupid bitch was still his wife, no matter what any judge had to say about it.

She thought she heard Jesse's name in there, but she was only half listening, her nerves quivering as she tried to figure out how she could make it out of there in one piece.

The man obviously wanted revenge, but she wasn't quite sure how she fit into the whole picture. Though she didn't really want to know, she figured the more information she had to rely on, the better her chances of surviving.

She thought of Jesse and the weekend they'd shared, the bright color he had brought to her cold, gray world. She wanted to be in his arms again, to feel wonderfully, miraculously whole again. To tell him how very much she loved him.

She was going to have to survive, no matter what.

"What are you planning to do with me?" She interrupted Sylvester's rambling with a calmness that belied the panic surging through her veins.

He blinked at her in surprise—just as if the chair he was sitting on had suddenly started carrying on a conversation—then suddenly smirked at her over the lip of the nearly empty Jack Daniel's bottle. "You're gonna help me, Teach."

"How?"

"See this?" He held up the gun with a broad smile. "This here belongs to Seth Son-of-a-Bitch Garrett. Registered and everything. Who do you think's gonna get blamed when it happens to be used to commit a crime?"'

"Seth?"

"Give the teacher an A-plus." He saluted her with the bottle.

Keep him talking. Talking and drinking, until Jesse had time to get there or until he passed out, so she could escape.

"How did you get the gun?"

Sylvester grinned at his own cleverness. "Wasn't hard. I made my boy give me the key to their fancy house so I could get in whenever I wanted. They never even knew I'd been there. Not like at your house. I didn't even get close before you saw me and called the police."

She thought of the intruder, that dark, menacing shape outside her window. "That was you?"

He snickered but didn't answer.

"Why me?"

"You dropped right into my lap, sugar." He seemed to have a little trouble getting the words out and she prayed he was too drunk to notice as she casually stretched her leg out and pretended to shift positions while she carefully slid a thick, five-inch-long shard of glass from the shattered coin jar closer, hiding it under her shoe.

"My kid said you and our pretty-boy police chief were close. Thought I'd see if he was tellin' me more lies. For once he was right. The minute you saw me, you called him, didn't you?"

"He's the police chief. Of course I called him."

"Aw, come on. You don't have to fool ol' Hob Sylvester. You're doin' him, aren't you?"

She flushed at his crudeness. *Keep him talking. Even if you don't like what he's saying.* "What does that have to do with anything?"

"When I saw you, I came up with a great idea. Kill two birds with one stone, you know, and make them both pay for screwing up my life. While I'm setting up that son of a bitch Garrett to take the fall when you're found shot to death with his gun, I can also make Jesse Harte bleed by taking away something of his. It's the least I can do for my old football buddy." His cold smile oozed hatred.

"What did Jesse do to you?"

"Ruined my life, that's what he did!" He threw the empty bottle against the wall suddenly and she shuddered at the crash. "If it wasn't for him, I would have played college ball and maybe even the pros. I was one hell of a wide receiver. Had colleges knockin' down my door. University of Wyoming, Colorado. UNLV. They all wanted Hob Sylvester on their roster, I'll tell you what. Then Jesse Harte had to go and ruin it for me."

"How?" she whispered.

"Last game of the regular season, scouts in the stands, and QB hotshot Harte decides to blow off the game. He didn't even show up! How was I supposed to let the scouts see what I could do when I had that wussy Troy Smoot throwing for me?''

She didn't understand half of what he was saying. Football wasn't exactly one of her areas of expertise, but besides that, his words began to slur.

She cursed her stupid knee. If not for that, she could probably easily outrun a man who was more than half-drunk, even down a slippery mountainside.

Jesse, please hurry.

''Him and Garrett and that bitch I married are in it together. And now they have to pay. That's all. You just made the mistake of getting messed up with the wrong guy, sugar.''

He was crazy. He had to be if he thought this ridiculous plan would actually work, that anyone would blame Seth Garrett for her death.

''Guess we might as well get to it, right?'' He lifted the gun and she couldn't help flinching.

''Here? You're going to kill me here, now?''

''Why not?''

She drew a shaky breath, scrambling for an answer. In the end, she decided to play to his ego. ''Seems to me a smart man like you would realize the police would never believe Seth would bring me out here to kill me,'' she pointed out. ''All the clues except the gun will point to you. Your fingerprints have to be all over this place.''

He scratched his head. ''So where should we go?''

She had the sudden, hysterical urge to laugh. Was the man actually drunk—or insane—enough to think she was going to give him a blueprint for her own murder? ''Where would Mayor Garrett do it?''

His big, dissipated face suddenly brightened. ''I

know. The courthouse. The sumbitch practically lives there. Come on, let's go.''

He gestured with the gun toward the door. Her time was running out.

Sarah pretended to stumble as she rose, and staggered to her knees. While still down, she quickly closed her fist around the thick glass shard, heedless of it slicing through her skin.

As her fingers folded around the sharp, cold glass, a strange, empowering strength flowed through her. She might go down in the end, but this time she would go down fighting, damn it.

She stayed on the ground for several seconds, until Sylvester turned toward her, snarling impatiently. ''Come on. Hurry up.''

It wasn't hard to make a distressed noise. ''My knee. I have problems with it sometimes. I don't think I can get up.''

He muttered a harsh curse. ''You better not be faking,'' he warned, but stretched a hand out to help her up.

He brushed her breast as he reached for her. If not for that, she might not have had the courage, but in that moment he became Tommy DeSilva. All her hatred toward what had been done to her focused on him.

With a grunt of rage, she drew her hand back and aimed for his eyes with all her strength.

With a scream of pain, Sylvester backed away, clutching at his face. Bile rose in her throat at the sight of him, like something out of a horror movie—the glass shard sticking out of one eye, blood pouring everywhere.

She nearly collapsed right then as the past jerked back to the present, but she knew she wasn't safe. Not while he still had a gun. With one hand she snagged the keys to the truck off the counter where he'd left them and raced out the door as fast as her knee would allow.

Half skidding, half jumping, she made her way down the slippery steps and was almost to the truck when a wild shot rang out behind her. She didn't take time to look, just leapt for the cab of the truck, then fumbled with both locks.

She wasted a few scary moments trying to figure out which key would start the truck, then she jammed the right one in. It worked! The truck rumbled to life just as another shot rang out, shattering the passenger window. Sarah didn't wait around anymore. She muscled the truck into gear, thanking heaven her father had bothered to teach her how to drive a manual, then roared through the darkness.

She was halfway down the mountain, trying her best to drive with shaking hands and tears of shock running down her face, when she heard the first siren.

Chapter 13

"Okay. Twelve stitches down, just a few more to go. Can you hang in there?"

Sarah nodded at the short, competent doctor with the steel-gray buzz cut and kind blue eyes behind wire-rimmed glasses. She had never been treated by a doctor wearing a bolo tie before.

"Good girl." He smiled and hunched back over her palm to continue repairing the damage she had done to herself by wielding a broken shard of glass with her bare hand.

"How's the pain?" the nurse asked.

Numb. Just like the rest of her. She had novocaine where her emotions, where her soul, were supposed to be. "Fine." She mustered a smile. "Can't feel a thing."

"Let me know when it starts to wear off," Dr. Wallace said. "We can give you another shot."

She nodded. All she wanted to do was close her eyes

for a while and pretend the past two hours had never happened. But the white-coated professionals at the Salt River Health Clinic wouldn't give her that luxury. Not when there was poking and prodding and bandaging to be done.

It didn't really matter. She doubted if she would be able to forget, even for a moment. Lucky her—she now had a lovely assortment of nightmares to choose from each night.

Besides, what she *really* wanted was Jesse's arms around her once more, for him to gather her up against that broad, hard chest and hold her there forever.

The few fleeting moments after he yanked her out of Hob Sylvester's battered pickup and into his arms had been the only time she'd felt completely safe since she had walked out to her car after school.

She had sobbed with relief as he held her fiercely. It was over. Jesse was there and everything would be okay.

But the embrace had been brief. After making sure she wasn't seriously injured, he had handed her off to Officer Hernandez with terse instructions to take Sarah to the clinic while he dealt with Sylvester.

The doctor stopped stitching at her sudden frown. "Are the shots wearing off? Are you regaining feeling?"

"No. I was just...I was wondering how he is. Sylvester."

The kindness vanished from the doctor's eyes. Instead they looked flinty, angry. Not at her, she realized, but at the man who had wreaked such havoc in her life and others.

"Last report I had, the chopper crew had him stabilized," he answered. "The doctors at the University of Utah will take care of him. Who knows, they might even be able to save the sight in that eye. Won't do him much good in prison, though, and that's exactly where the sleazebag is headed.''

As Chris Hernandez drove her to the clinic, the police radio in her vehicle had squawked the entire time. Through the crisp communications, Sarah learned that Hob Sylvester had surrendered to Jesse and county sheriff's deputies without a fight, in too much agony from his injury to stage much of the fuss she suspected Jesse had been hoping for.

She closed her eyes, trying to block the memory of that terrible moment when she had lunged toward him with that glass shard. Another nightmare to add to her list.

She wouldn't regret it, though. She had only been protecting herself, had done what she had to. If she ever did have a twinge of guilt at possibly causing a man to lose the sight in one eye, all she had to do was remember Corey and his bruises and the gruesome, obscene mark of ownership his own father had left scarred into his back.

''Okay.'' Dr. Wallace tied off the last stitch. ''We're all done here.''

''May I go home now?''

''I don't have any reason to keep you any longer. Do you have a ride home?''

''Yes. I'll take her.''

At that deep, rough voice, Sarah's gaze flew to the door of the exam room. Jesse filled the doorway. An ugly smear of blood on the shoulder of his uniform gave her a bad moment, until she realized it was her own, from that brief time he had held her.

She almost flew into his arms right then, but checked

the impulse. She could hang on for a few more minutes, just until they were alone.

If she hadn't already restrained herself, the look in his eyes would have done the job.

He looked wild. As if fierce violence seethed just under his skin. In another man, she might have found that raw energy terrifying, but not with Jesse. In him, it was only unsettling.

"Are there any precautions she needs to take once she's out of here?" he asked the doctor.

"Just use common sense. Keep the bandage dry and change it a few times every day."

"What about something for the pain?"

Sarah shook her head. "I don't want anything. I'll be fine."

The doctor shrugged. "You heard the lady. She can take over-the-counter pain relief if necessary, or if the pain intensifies, give me a call and I'll write out a scrip."

The doctor and nurse walked out of the exam room, leaving the two of them alone. Sarah waited for Jesse to pull her into his arms at last. Instead he stood by the door, his features stony and hard. "Are you ready?" he asked gruffly.

"I...yes. Please, take me home."

A few moments later, Jesse had bundled her up and ushered her out to his waiting patrol vehicle, all without touching her once.

Baffled and hurt by his distance, she sat quietly in the passenger seat, listening to the tires humming on the wet road and the staticky voices on the scanner. What was wrong? What had she done to make him so angry?

"I'm going to have to ask you some questions," he

finally said when they were a few blocks from her house. "Do you want to answer them tonight or in the morning?"

She frowned at his formal tone and wrapped her hands tightly around herself, trying to contain the chill spreading through her. What was wrong? What had she done?

"Tonight," she murmured. "I have school tomorrow."

"Don't you ever get a substitute?"

"When I need it. I won't need one tomorrow. I'm sure I'll be fine in the morning."

He was quiet for several moments, his mouth in a tight line. "I didn't think you would want to be alone," he finally said, "so I arranged for Cassie to stay the night with you. She's probably at your house now."

I wouldn't be alone if you stayed with me, she almost said. *If you stay and hold me and keep me warm.* She choked down the words. How could she say them when he obviously had gone to a great deal of trouble to fix things so he wouldn't have to stay with her?

He didn't want to be alone with her. She might still feel shocky and rattled, but she could figure out that much.

Where was the sexy, laughing man who had spent the night with her? Who couldn't seem to touch her enough over the two days? Who had awakened her by blowing raspberries on her stomach and had explored every inch of her skin with his powerful hands? Who had looked at her with a soft, aching tenderness glinting in his blue eyes?

Somehow between this morning when she had left his arms and tonight, that man had disappeared. This Jesse was a stranger, abrupt and distant and withdrawn.

''It was nice of Cassie to agree to stay,'' she murmured, staring out the windshield at the wet road glistening in the headlights.

''She's worried about you. I'm sure she could stay a few nights or more if you need her to.''

He pulled into her driveway and turned off the engine but made no move to climb out. For the first time she saw the lines of strain around his mouth, the muscle clenching in his jaw, the wildness that turned his blue eyes dark and murky. He looked like a man just barely holding on to control.

She swallowed hard and gathered courage. If she could take on a man with a gun, surely she could confront the man she loved. ''Jesse, what is it? Why are you so upset?''

Some of his fury bubbled out and the look he aimed at her was razor sharp. ''Why the hell do you think I'm upset? You could have been killed tonight!''

She drew a deep, shuddering breath, remembering those terrible moments when she thought she would never see him again. ''But I wasn't. I survived, Jesse.''

''No thanks to me. I should have been able to protect you. It was my job to keep you safe and I let Sylvester waltz right in and take you. Hell, I practically handed you to him on a silver platter.''

''Your job? Is that all it was?''

He didn't answer. In the dim moonlight she saw that muscle clench in his jaw again, but he didn't say anything. In the awful, drawn-out silence, she wondered if he was able to hear the crack and shatter of her heart.

She was a fool. She had begun to build stupid, silly fantasies of forever with a man who didn't know the meaning of the word. Who had probably slept with her out of pity and obligation, only because she had practically begged him to.

"I changed my mind," she said quietly, opening the door of the Bronco. "I don't think I want to answer any questions tonight. Now I think I would just like to go inside and sleep."

"Sarah—"

She shook her head. *Go away. Go away before I break apart.* "Good night, Jess."

Clutching her bandaged hand against her heart, she walked slowly, carefully into her house on old, tired bones.

Sometimes being clean and sober really sucked.

Right about now, Jesse would give just about anything for a good, stiff drink. Or two or three or ten. And it was only eight-frigging-thirty in the morning.

He had one mother of a headache squeezing his skull like a junkyard compactor. That's what happened when he tried to keep going for twenty-four hours on no sleep and way too much coffee.

The words and spaces on the incident forms in front of him all blurred together into one big gray mess and he blinked, trying to focus. It was a futile effort. How was he supposed to fill out the necessary paperwork of Sylvester's arrest when he couldn't concentrate on anything but fragmented, tortured images from the evening before?

The cold clutch of terror in his stomach at finding out Hob Sylvester had taken Sarah.

That terrible moment when he had pulled her, bleeding and sobbing, from that ratty pickup truck and into his arms.

Finding out from a ranting Sylvester that Jesse

couldn't live down his past, that it was an intrinsic part of his present—that one of the reasons Hob had targeted her, put her through a hell Jesse couldn't even begin to imagine, was because of him. Twisted revenge for some stupid thing he'd done sixteen years ago, in those awful, reckless months after his parents died.

The last image in his mind was the worst—the shattered hurt in Sarah's big green eyes right before she walked away from him.

He had wounded her. She had needed things from him the night before that he had been unable to offer.

He hadn't meant to hurt her, hadn't wanted to, but on some level he supposed it had been inevitable. Sooner or later she would figure out she deserved better.

His sweet Sarah.

His chest ached suddenly and the words swam before his eyes. Not his. She had never been his. He had been fooling himself to think a man with a hell-raising past could hold on to something so good.

He scrubbed his hands over his face and forced himself to turn back to the paperwork. He was on a short clock here—he would have to leave soon if he was going to make the five-hour drive to Salt Lake City to interrogate Sylvester in the hospital.

And wouldn't it be a treat trying to spend five minutes in the same room with the bastard without breaking him into tiny little pieces?

There had been more than a few moments the night before when he'd been tempted to indulge in a little police brutality while he arrested the son of a bitch. For Sarah. For Ginny. For Corey. The only thing stopping him had been the honor of his badge and the very real fear that if he started, he wouldn't be able to stop.

His phone suddenly buzzed and Lou's gravelly voice gritted over his intercom. "Boss, you have company coming in."

"Not now, Lou. I'm busy. Just tell 'em I'm not here."

"Too late." His little sister stalked into his office, her eyes a dark, stormy blue and a fierce scowl on her face.

"You're an idiot," Cassie snapped. "Did I ever tell you that?"

He did not need a confrontation with her today. He leaned back in his chair. "Good to see you, too, sis. And yes, I believe you've mentioned that a time or two."

"What the hell is wrong with you?"

I need a drink. And a woman I can't have. "What *isn't* wrong?" he murmured.

She shook her head in disgust. "Would you like me to round up a few puppies you can drop-kick, too, just for laughs? Because that's exactly what you did to Sarah last night."

"I didn't do anything!"

"Yeah, that's the point, isn't it? She needed comfort. She needed to feel safe. She needed you, you big idiot! And you just ditched her like you were some kind of cabbie dropping off a fare."

"It wasn't like that," he muttered.

"What was it like?" His little sister didn't get mad very often. She had always been the calm one in the family, the peacemaker, but right now she churned with fury, like some vast, storm-tossed ocean.

At his continued silence, she shook her head in disgust. "You don't get it, do you? For some mysterious reason the woman is crazy in love with you, Jess. I've seen the two of you together, I've seen the way you look at her and I know her feelings are not one-sided.''

''You don't know anything about this.''

''Maybe not. But I have seen you with plenty of women over the years. Too damn many, if you ask me.''

''I didn't ask you,'' he muttered.

She went on as if she hadn't heard him. ''And never once have you looked at any of them the same way you look at Sarah. You want to tell me why, then, you ran off when she needed you more last night than she's probably ever needed anyone in her life?''

''I had things to do. Loose ends to tie up, just like I do now,'' he said, with a pointed look at the paperwork scattered across his desk.

''And those loose ends were more important than Sarah?''

''No. But I had a job to do. If I had focused on that job in the first place, none of it would have happened.''

He hadn't meant to say that. Not to Cassie, who knew him too damn well. She stared at him, then her eyes narrowed. ''This is why you didn't stay when she needed you last night? Because you think it's your fault Sylvester got to her?''

He didn't answer. He didn't need to.

''You're an even bigger idiot than I thought,'' she snapped.

''Just back off, Cass. This is none of your business.''

''It is my business when two people I care about are hurting. You're not responsible for what Hob Sylvester did, Jess.''

''No. But I was responsible for keeping Sarah safe, and I failed.''

She came around to his side of the desk and perched

on the edge of it. After a moment spent studying him, she sighed. "This is about what happened with Mom and Dad, isn't it?"

He opened his mouth to argue, then closed it again. The night before, he had experienced the same grim helplessness he had felt climbing up the mountainside after the accident. Knowing his parents were down there dying while he tried to claw his way to help. Knowing his father probably would have seen that patch of black ice and been able to avoid it if he hadn't been arguing with him at the time.

Knowing he couldn't fix this, that he would have to live with the harsh guilt of failure for the rest of his life.

All those feelings and more had plowed through him the night before as he had rushed after Sarah.

Once more he had failed to save someone he loved.

"Oh, Jess." Cassie must have read all those things in his face. She touched his cheek tenderly and he had to fight the urge to wrap his arms around his little sister and cry like a baby.

After a moment, she cleared her throat. "None of it was your fault. Not Mom and Dad's accident and not what happened to Sarah."

"I should have been able to keep her safe."

Cassie shook her head. "You can't save the whole world, Jess."

"I didn't need to save the whole world. Just Sarah."

Cassie was quiet for a moment, then she spoke softly. "Did it ever occur to you that maybe this time she needed to rescue herself? If only to prove to herself that she could?"

He stared at her, struck speechless by her words. By her wisdom.

Why hadn't he seen it? He had been so consumed with guilt at not saving Sarah, at letting Sylvester get to her, that he hadn't thought about how empowering it must have been for Sarah to fight back against Sylvester when she was threatened this time.

To fight back and to win.

He thought of her attack in Chicago. Where on earth had she found the kind of courage to defend herself against Sylvester, especially when she knew the consequences better than anyone else? When she had lived through those very consequences and still had the scars to prove it, both physical and emotional.

A hot, fierce pride settled in his heart. His brave Sarah.

"I'm no expert in this area," Cassie went on. "Heaven knows, I've made a mess of my own life. But I have the feeling the two of you could share something special. Something rare and precious. Don't let the past get in the way of your future."

She was right. That was exactly what he was doing. He was throwing away the best thing that had ever happened to him because he was afraid. If Sarah could be brave enough to fight for her life, couldn't he be brave enough to fight for his?

Yes. Hell, yes.

"Thanks, brat." He kissed her forehead, then headed for the door.

"Where are you going?" she asked.

He grinned, his first smile since the afternoon before, when he had seen Sarah's empty car. "School. It looks like I still have a few things to learn."

Chapter 14

She had a feeling it was going to be a very difficult day. School had been in session for only an hour and she already felt exhausted, as wrung out as a wet, soapy dishrag.

Maybe she should have found a substitute today. With only another two weeks of school before summer vacation, her students were wired, wriggling around in their seats and chattering incessantly.

After the trauma of the day before and a night spent staring at the ceiling—longing for something she couldn't have—she wasn't sure she had the energy to keep up with them.

On the other hand, she had only a few more days with her class and she hated to miss a minute of it.

Right now their restlessness had been moderately contained while they painted watercolors under Janie Parker's instruction, but she feared the brief respite wouldn't last.

"Miss McKenzie?"

She glanced up to find Corey standing at her desk, shifting from foot to foot. The boy had been wary around her since school started, giving her furtive, watchful looks all morning.

She knew she would have to talk to him at some point about what had happened the day before, about what his father had done to both of them, but she didn't want to push him. He would talk to her when he was ready.

And it looked as if the time was now. "Hi," she said softly.

He swallowed hard. "I, um, I made you a picture." He held it out. "The paint's still a little wet."

"Thank you, Corey!" Touched beyond words, she took it carefully, treating it like the treasured prize it was. "This is really lovely."

"I know you like flowers and stuff. That's what it is."

Her heart crested, overflowed, and she felt the hot sting of tears. "I can see. You're very good, Corey. When it dries, I'll have it framed and hang it on my wall so I can look at it and be in a garden anytime I want. Even in the middle of winter."

He gave her a small, pleased smile, but she could tell he was still troubled. He stood there chewing on his lip for several moments. She waited patiently, knowing he would get around to it sooner or later.

"I'm real sorry about what happened to you, Miz McKenzie." He finally blurted out the words all in a rush.

Tears shimmered in his eyes. "It's my fault he took you. I should have told someone he was back. He told me not to, but I shouldn't have listened. If I had told, Chief Harte might have found him before he hurt you.''

He sniffled, then one tear slid down through his freckles, then another and another. She couldn't bear his distress any longer. Teary herself, she gathered him against her. ''Shhh. Sweetheart, it's okay. None of it was your fault. I know it wasn't your fault.''

''I didn't want to see him anymore, but he made me. Said I was a Sylvester, too, and I needed to spend time with my old man. I thought he would hurt my mom or Maddie if I didn't go.''

''I know.''

He swiped at his eyes with his sleeve and she handed him a tissue. ''Do you hate me now because I was too chicken to tell and lied about everything? About Hob taking the school quarters and the mark on my back and everything else?''

''Oh, Corey. No. Of course not.'' How could she tell him she knew all too well what it was to share your life with the snarling creature fear could be? ''On the contrary. I'm very proud of you. Even though you were afraid of your father, you finally did the right thing last night and told Chief Harte where to find me. It was a very brave thing to do.''

He colored and looked down at her desk, mumbling a denial. She smiled at the top of his head. She had been right about Corey. Inside this troubled, rebellious child lurked a sweet boy who painted flowers for his teacher because he knew she liked them.

''So we're still friends?'' Corey asked.

''The best,'' she assured him. ''Now, why don't you take your seat again for the rest of art class?''

He nodded. With a watery smile he turned and started to return to his seat, then froze, his head turned toward the doorway of the class. Sarah followed his gaze and her heart began a fierce, slow rhythm.

Jesse's broad shoulders filled the door frame. He wore his police uniform, complete with Stetson and sidearm, and he looked big and masculine and wonderful. Her love for him was a thick, heavy ache in her chest.

He was watching Corey and she held her breath, praying Jesse wouldn't ruin the progress she had just made with the boy, that he wouldn't be angry with him for the secrets he had been forced to keep.

She should have known better. Jesse's expression held no condemnation. Though he said nothing, the look he shared with Corey was warm and approving. The boy basked in it. As he walked the rest of the way to his desk, his shoulders were a little bit straighter, his head a little higher.

Jesse's gaze returned to her and Sarah felt heat crawl up her cheekbones. She thought of the vast chasm between them the night before, the cold distance he had placed between them. Her emotions were already so ragged she wasn't sure she could endure more this morning.

He opened his mouth to speak to her, but before he could, Dylan and Lucy spied their uncle. They rushed to him, chattering eagerly. He returned their hugs, but his gaze never left Sarah's face as he bent his head to speak to the girls.

From her desk at the other side of the room, she couldn't hear more than the murmur of his low voice, but the girls' eyes widened. They looked at him, then back at their teacher with such amazed expressions that she could only wonder with a little clutch of apprehension what he had said to them.

The girls rushed back to their seats and Jesse straightened. The noisy bustle of her classroom seemed to fade into a dull murmur, leaving just the two of them.

"Miz McKenzie, may I speak with you out in the hall?"

Please. She couldn't break down in the middle of class. She cast her eyes around the classroom looking for an excuse and found Janie watching them both, her expression filled with avid curiosity.

"Go, Sarah," the art teacher said. "I've got everything covered in here."

Thanks for nothing. Left with no alternative, she rose slowly from her desk and followed him out into the hall, steeling her heart against more of this painful reserve.

"This really isn't a good time for me to give a statement," she said when the door was closed firmly behind her. "Could we do it after school?"

"I'm not here to take your statement."

"No?"

He shook his head but didn't elaborate, just watched her out of those blue eyes that saw entirely too much. Could he tell she had stayed up most of the night silently weeping over him? Over her own foolishness in offering her heart to a man who didn't want it?

She sincerely hoped not.

"How's your hand?" he asked.

Whatever she thought he might say, she hadn't expected that. "I...fine. Showering was a little tricky, but I managed. It's a little sore, but nothing I can't handle."

"I know. Have I ever told you how your ability to

cope with anything life throws at you never ceases to amaze?''

How was she supposed to answer that? Flustered, she looked down at her bandaged hand, then back into his blue eyes that watched her so steadily. ''I'm sorry, Jesse. Art class will be over in a few moments and I have to get back to my class. If you're not here for a statement, how can I help you?''

''By forgiving me.''

She blinked at him, stunned by the intensity of his words. ''There's nothing to forgive.''

''As my baby sister so bluntly informed me this morning, I was an idiot last night.''

Had Cassie heard her weeping last night from the guest room? She must have, even though Sarah had tried fiercely to muffle her sobs with her pillow. Mortified heat soaked her cheeks and she swallowed hard, focusing her gaze on the brown carpet. ''It doesn't matter.''

''It matters to me. I hurt you. I would give anything to take it back, but I can't.''

He was quiet for a long time, until she finally had to look up, to meet his glittering blue gaze. He reached for her hand, the bandaged one, and held it tenderly. ''My only excuse is that I've never been in love before.''

She stared at him. ''What did you say?''

''I said I've never been in love before.''

''And you...you are now?''

He smiled. ''Don't sound so shocked, sweetheart. Why do you think I've been acting like an idiot? A certain schoolteacher I know is tying me up in knots inside.''

She looked so astonished by the idea—then so intrigued—that if he hadn't already realized he loved her, he would have tumbled headfirst right then.

"I love you, Sarah," he murmured.

There. That wasn't so bad. Would her face go all soft, her eyes all bright, every time he said it? He couldn't wait to find out.

She sniffled. "You do?"

"Completely."

"Why?"

He laughed outright. "You're not supposed to ask me why. You're just supposed to accept it."

"How would you know? You said you've never done this before."

She had a point there. "Okay. Why do I love you? Because you're sweet and brave and wonderful and you make me feel like a better person when I'm with you."

There were stars in her eyes when she murmured his name, and he couldn't stand it any more. He had to kiss her.

"Wait," she said when he bent his head.

Jesse groaned and rested his forehead against hers. "You're killing me here, sweetheart. Do you need more reasons why I love you? There's plenty more where those came from. It just might take me a minute. I'm afraid I'm not thinking too clearly right now."

She shook her head, laughing a little at his disgruntled tone. "Later, maybe. I just wanted you to know that I...I feel the same way."

"Good," he said, reaching for her again.

No. She couldn't get away that easily, she had to say the words. "I love you, Jesse Harte. Because you're kind and strong and wonderful, and you made me laugh when I didn't think I ever could again."

He gazed at her, his blue eyes dark with emotion, then he cleared his throat. "Now can I kiss you?"

She smiled and wrapped her arms around his neck. He swept her to him, then that hard, beautiful mouth was on hers, full of love and joy and promise. She forgot where they were, forgot the aching loss of the night before, forgot everything but the wonder of being in his arms.

"What is the meaning of this?"

She gasped at the interruption and would have pulled away, but Jesse held her tight, looking over her head at the principal. She watched that devil's smile take over and he spoke in the slow drawl he sometimes used. "Well, see, Chuck, it's called kissing and it can be a real kick when you're doing it with the right person."

He turned that slow, sexy smile in her direction and Sarah forgot to breathe.

The principal glared at both of them. "Yes, Chief Harte, I believe I know what kissing is. I also know it doesn't belong in the classroom."

Jesse just shrugged. "I guess that's why we're out in the hall, then, Chuck."

It took every ounce of control to hold on to her laughter while the principal tried to figure out how to answer that. Eventually he gave up, just returned to his office with a grunt, and her laughter bubbled out. "You are a troublemaker, Jesse Harte."

"I've been trying to tell you, I'm reformed. Haven't you been listening?" After a moment, his grin faded and a hint of uncertainty appeared in his eyes. "I've had a pretty wild past, Sarah. Done plenty of things I'm not proud of. I want you to know that up front."

And she had been to hell and back. And survived.

"The past doesn't matter," she said. "It's where we go from here that's important."

He swept her into his arms again. When he finally broke the kiss this time, they were both breathless.

"Um, looks like we've drawn a crowd." His voice came out strangled.

She glanced back at her classroom door and found most of her students peering at them through the small window. Lucy and Dylan were right in the front, their eyes huge and their mouths hanging open.

"I guess Chuck is right," Jesse muttered. "This really isn't the place for this."

She stared at him in astonishment. "You're blushing! I can't believe you're blushing!"

"Look what a terrible influence you are already!"

She laughed. "Don't change too much. See, I've got this thing for bad boys…"

For this one, anyway.

* * * * *